**a work by N. Casio Poe**

**{VOID}**

# BLUE YOLK

## a work by N. Casio Poe

**a work by N. Casio Poe**

**for David Britton, Isidore Lucien Ducasse, Richard McCaslin, and Tony Kiritsis.**

--------------------------------------------------------------

*there are some whose dread of human beings is so morbid they yearn to see monsters of even more horrible shapes.*

from *No Longer Human* by Osamu Dazai, adapted to manga by Junji Ito (pg. 60, Viz Media, 2020)

*the killer is no longer operating upon a recognizable basis of logic, and what he does to his victim before or after death is motivated by what can only be called magical thinking, where a private world of symbols and significance is acted out in psychodrama form upon the victim.*

from *From Hell: Master Edition* by Alan Moore (pg. 32 of Appendix 1, Top Shelf Publications, 1996, 2020)

--------------------------------------------------

{VOID}

JERK CURTAIN.

spotlight hits a woman's face.

spotlight widens... the woman's aquamarine hair frames her stern countenance in a hacked-up thicket of ocean weeds and gelatinous algae.

spotlight widens. the woman has an infant loaded in a front-facing baby carrier, which is strapped to her chest. the look on the infant's face is even more sour than that of the woman... surgery from repairs to a cleft palate creating a deep V shaped hairlip, which the infant can't resist filling with their spittle-lacquered tongue.

spotlight widens... the carrier is wrapped in soft putty-grey bricks, each indented with a crest that resembles a flower with an egg-shaped rodent skull in the bud.

spotlight widens.... a cylindrical remote is being gripped in the woman's left hand.

spotlight widens... rubbery blue cables snake in a braid from the bottom of the remote, splitting off into tendrils that sink their narrow copper frameworks into the cadaver-scale tar of the bricks that have been strapped to the baby carrier.

spotlight widens.... as the under-knuckle of her thumb strokes the candy-red button of the remote, the woman places her right hand atop the infant's head, lightly tussling its gossamer whisps.

{VOID}

spotlight widens.... failing to outpace the radius of the blast.

spotlight settles on the calming fall of woman and child as their pulped shrapnel runs down the center of a large emblem painted on the wall that was previously obscured by their presence; a much more ornate version of the crest that indented the semi-hard clay of the explosives. innumerable grey knives arranged into a blooming rose, its bud a wet looking skinned rat head, ocular sockets loaded with a grid of eyes, its mouth filled with the letters S, V, an K crabbed together to the point of appearing from a distance like a strip of Xs, its meat and gore the blue of a fading bruise.

"so Sirhan Sirhan creampies a rolled-up *Steven Universe* duvet while snorting a line of Roman Reign's leukemia dingle berries off of Caylee Anthony's pelvic mound."

"oh i get it."

*They bend SHOSHANA back in a smoke ring produced by the BBQ grill's tearing stones. When they force her to arch her spine, she flips her hair like an old time starlet.*

*The children are waiting in line to punch SHOSHANA in the face. She smiles with cracked euphoria between every blow from a child's fist. Her joy-envenomed countenance becomes swollen and black-toothed, a cruel hiss of air wheezing from her crooked nose, its shape changing like mountains cut by waves. A boy kicks a football into the left side of her head, which thuds off the temple and pangs onto the burning grill. The force of the blow pushed her eyeball out of the socket, but only slightly. The stalk of the eye gets pinned between the inflating lids. The eyeball wells up with almond milk. Her steel-wool eyebrows are dusted with the peach-leavings of dozens of erasers being furiously rubbed on the roofs of the nearby homes, brushed off by the air of swooping hands.*

*A puddle of black coffee gathers in the gutter of SHOSHANA's back, turning cobalt from the sweat and skin. The ghostly reflection of an astral-projected child molester is rippled in all but its teeth. It begins to circle as if being inhaled by a drain, but the pond remains full.*

*an Underside tulpa named HADASSAH SIVICK; SHOSHANA's static-eyed doppelganger, writhes in a cough-medicine-drenched serpentine all around the balled-fisted children. HADASSAH's hair is the reverse of SHOSHANA's hair; mostly black with hints of blond instead of mostly blond with hints of black. SHOSHANA has grey streaks whereas HADASSAH has silver. Though still relatively youthful, portions of their skin hangs like crushed velvet in soft, ribbed clumps. Her entire nude body is a violet checkerboard of abrasions. She opens the lipped-valve at the top of her throat, which erupts in white noise and blenders that somehow makes her hair spark copper.*

*A plastic baggie packed with nail clippings is propping up the SHOSHANA's skinny feet.*

*HADASSAH crouches down and opens the baggie, ferreting through the clipping. She feels around for the big toe nails. When she has gathered roughly ten of them, she turns her attention to SHOSHANA's rear end. HADASSAH begins to place the big toe nails in the grooves of SHOSHANA's anus.*

*"You're going to like it. it'll feel like a cat trying to pull you open and crawl inside."*

*At least that's what it sounded like HADASSAH said through the orchestral whirring of grounded polyps she calls a voice.*

*When HADASSAH is finished, SHOSHANA's asshole looks like an outsider artist's sun bleached metal sculpture of a daisy. The doppelganger's nose attempts to pollinate the rectum, but to no avail. HADASSAH perches up her face to suggest the sour, clasping and reclasping her hand while lightly stomping her feet.*

*The football has completely melted on the grill, the bright brown rubber smothering charred hamburgers, cutting bubbled stars into the ruined meat. The lace is like a white caterpillar curled on a disc of sun. a rodent-faced midget hops in a circle around the grill, further fanning the smoke.*

*HADASSAH snaps a water balloon on each one of her gnarled nipples. She lactates into them, filling them to such a capacity that they become a cartoonish exaggeration of her own breasts. The disproportionate features of leering nightmare faces are vibrating on the pink domes, forecasting a hemorrhoidal rupture. Milk escapes through the pinholes of their eyes, smoking when it hits the ground.*

*SHOSHANA's face is now a cauliflower globe. There is still a line of children waiting to get their hits. Her popped eyeball has almost been slurped back into the socket by the welts. HADASSAH dances to a steel guitar only she can hear, singing along with the karaoke cadence of a swarm of hornets.*

*The next child steps up to deliver a haymaker into SHOSHANA's bubbled skull. He's dressed in a black suit and tie, his face covered by sackcloth with electric tape Xs for his eyes. He cocks his burlap head, examining SHOSHANA's bulbous features. He pulls the sack over and off his head, revealing a tiny version of her own speedbag of a face; rocky with fisted knots that in silhouetted profile resembles the head of goat with horns that have been scalloped to approximate the membrane of a large bat's wings.*

*The slurping voice of this boy catches the attention of HADASSAH,, as if the record scratched on the voices in her head. She approaches the goat-headed child, crouches down to his level, and gently places her hands on his shoulders, slowly craning him toward her.*

*When HADASSAH speaks, her voice is now cleaned of all feedback choirs. What emerges is a whispery, sensual voice  that could either console or provoke.*

*"long eggs."*

*The goat headed boy, HADASSAH, SHOSHANA, and all the children at the party begin laughing a tape-popping backwards track of a laugh. Suddenly, HADASSAH is distracted by a vicious black metal song kicking in her brain.*

*HADASSAH points to a layered hole where her ear used to be, little blades of grass growing like hairs in the trauma. The children all gather around in hopes to hear the tune. In their strain, malformed slug-like rodent heads pop out from their mouths, slowly vomiting blue-grey film on their tongues.*

*"Have you met my son Seamus?"*

*From the mass of shocked children, the guest of honor stands out for the first time since the festivities began. A lean young man, bald cranium slicked with a layer of oil, robed in yolky paste that clumps in his stubble. He contorts his face into that of a rat-faced demon's snarling orgasm. Lights shift on him in an epileptic strobe. He pulls cones of slurried gore out of the scalps of the prone children, swallowing it through vertical ladder-shaped gashes his palms. After that, the children all follow his jittery gait, doing their best do adopt the mocking dread of his hellishly elastic skin. They stop in their tracks only to ravenously glower at one another in a so-crude-its-sophisticated form of communication.*

*SEAMUS SIVICK creepy-crawls to HADASSAH and SHOSHANA, who are packing up to leave. He pulls them by the backs of their hair and croaks this between smoke-lunged cackles;*

{VOID}

# "ScaVilKad VriS!"

... you open the window...

... you attempt to blink away the stubborn fluids that fog your eyes...

... you notice the sun is clearly up and out, but your room has yet to willingly receive this information, its resistance toward acceptance of the solar flare tinting your flesh a midnight blue...

... your fingernails comb this flesh for grit and film...

... you suckle at the rim of these fingernails, compressing their salt between your dry tongue and the raw roof of your mouth, slashed to ribbons by a late night binge of coarse sugar cereal, which you shoveled out of the box and into your mouth by the handful...

... you notice the contents of your room are still hazed with midnight blue...

... you're still maintaining marble notebooks; a habit you purloined as a moody teenager from the cinematic mythos of disaffected young men, be they self-tortured lover boys or in the service of something much darker...

... you're mostly utilizing the notebook app on your phone these days; nowhere near as aesthetically startling as the crabbed sub-legible cipher-crawl of your penmanship; where slashed reams of thought are herded elbow-to-tit in pregnant mob scenes that pour across the bordering margins, but you'll admit that the autocorrect feature is a nice touch...

Annihilating-ly gastric rot-belchers of dubious merit and questionable relevance commit unlistenable postulations of numb repugnance to the digitally rolling glitch ether. a sexless weirdo in Pogo the Clown make-up performs an extended serial killer cringe dance while backed by a needle-drop that was composed by a convicted child pornographer, and I'm just like "...eh".

would this be an example of going too soft or being too hard?

a heavy buildup of tenacious calculus behind their teeth had the hummer feeling as if my cock was fucking a mouth full of a chewed-up pretzel pieces.

did you make it this way?

breeder engineering. legacy failsafe. apocalyptic undoing's. perma-children of the ether-hoarding spite bloat. perpetually expanding doom-booms. dependency of wreckage-brained cripples. nursed from one bust to another. accumulating mother's phlegm. bulks and bundles tucked and puddled in the toad-smooth crawl ducts of peeled battery cheeks; flaws becoming the sum total of their identity with steadily ramping regularity.

microwaved iguana on a blanket made out of third trimester abortion residue and shredded fibers of the constitution secretly lives on a human eyeball diet.

Aubrey Aurilean asks if we can switch desks because hers is creaking at maximum volume. as i am one to instantaneously grant the request of a woman, particularly one who falls into the parameters of what i find appealing, i grant her this wish. as i also do not wish to sit in the creaky desk, as it will no doubt draw unwanted attentions toward me, i instead opt to occupy one that is of an unfortunate closeness to the front of the room, which further caverns my innate discomfort with my surroundings, notching the anxiousness upward.

a boy, more comfortable in their skin than i, secure in their status and confident in their mass appeal, finds a series of notes on separate sheets of paper that have been folded into each other, forming a thick square. when the pages are unfolded, the contents of the notes reveal an outline for the heat death of a popular superhero universe.

these notes are mine.

he feigns interest and impression with my work, but once i am removed from the conversation and he resituates himself with those among the elite tier of his seemingly vast crowd, he settles into a state of cold mockery, of which the horde is eager to indulge.

the blackboard is crowded with a series of underground band logos. the conductor makes it a point to speak of his time spent in the street punk scene, to which a woman asks "do people like that?". in a bid to forge a connection with the conductor, i low-talk about my extended period in the grindcore scene, which is of relevance to the interest and curiosity of no one, not even who i assumed were of the prurient and the morbid.

opera-gloved in spunk lather... psoriatic harlequin being cut-fucked by gorgeous skeleton boys... their night-urines dark like tea... rim of the sprout blackened by insect carcass mash.

meth lab houseboats. grunt preamble. on all fours in mall lingerie.

I've got my inner child on suicide watch. amoebas maturate in a wash tub full of bowel obstructions, enema spillage dried and puffed into packing peanuts.

{VOID}

endocrine projectile. neural network hook suspension. wits' end vomiting thumbtacks, malnourished from a crash diet of ambient seasonal gasses.

degrees of a bad place. depravity's alluring freedom. inevitable cringe braces its orgasm, skittering rakes across the levering back.

manifesto back channel. a bedpan full of mosquitos grazing contact microphones. corpulent serial fondlers toast their mongoloid palms in the dumpster crackle, made further ugly by this blazing drag. have a nice last days of humanity.

Had a dream this morning that I play-strangled Aubrey Aurilean with a shredded death metal tee until they made a noise like a sputtering bandsaw.

in the worlds of my head, there is nothing unique.

fermenting plastic horses in waste bins filled with rat water. a cephalopod dildo where the tentacles are the straps so it looks as if their cunt is being engulfed by a baby squid.

floaters staining bedroom ceiling. horizon filtered through fogging goggle. pillory gait buckled at the throat. facing backward on a chair frame of steel pipe work. elbows over pipe. hands cuffed to spreader bar around back of head. lush-faced and groan-cadenced, limiting cognizance broken by the inches of a barrel-chested murder clown.

louse polyps. starch-golem. tonight's girlfriend metal armored for disappointment. prophylactic hatchling mitigates a threesome between a zip-tie, a trestle, and a velvet duvet in the white room where my children fall out windows.

feels like we're going backward, don't it? tip-toeing ass first into arranged marriages. forced to fend for a lifetime through a buzzsaw gauntlet of giant weird baby people just for the county fair  badge that reads of another night where you didn't have to cum alone.

female imprisonment comedy. the act enriched. the wanting deranged. teeth on teeth. birdshot facial scrub. spooning flayed hog backs on the cutter block of hybrist-ophilic triads. pervert cancer romantically dehydrated, the florid bloom of undergirding panics oxidized to a noble rot in the yawning why.

camouflage pattern of long birthmarks. a mirrored ossuary transmits the harem scolds braiding their vegetation. they whisper "the brine is blinking" to the rictus spat of the secreters' gleam, surreptitiously raiding the woman's hamper. as for the question of power electronics vs. pornogrind, that depends upon the thief's intention. if it was just for a giggle (however admittedly over the line), that's pornogrind. if it was because he wants his authenticity-obsessed peer-group to believe he's some kind of arch-level decadent who is strongly resistant to the notion of personal space when it comes to the those within orbit of his hermetic passions, then that's power electronics.

check my pulse tonight. a grave is just what i needed. hornets' nest formed around a mask in the shed. wet paint across the lower half of their face resembles a skeleton mouth of barcodes. designed this way to leave a branding upon the asshole they eat.

you know what's a good baby name? Truvada.

YEAH? WHAT IF COCK BALLS EVERYWHERE SENT PHOTOS OF MY ASSHOLE GRANDMOTHER? PENIS DOG THAT!

shartyrs. mercurial obstinance. blackout VCRs under the violet walls made out of ironed trash bags. Arizona Bae daylight robbing frozen cylinders of cattle semen.

strychnine boilermaker. current mud. choke-anchored by the debilitating struggle to maintain hideous friendships if only to fruitlessly resist the inevitable misanthropic pessimism that ceaselessly lurches within the blunt reality of my terminal personhood. this is the year of the scold.

aside from road rage piss-shouting, haven't used vocal cords in two years. it all keeps slowly changing for the worst. no imagination. no passion. no community. just terminally cynical old heads who are ceaselessly resistant toward anything new and lippy teenagers too eager to flex and talk shit (which they learned by watching the aforementioned old heads). a lot of sneering and bloat with no creative fortitude behind it, just floating husks meaninglessly engraved with muddy tattoos and unreadable patchwork who depend on the endeavors of others to fill in the blank of their identity yet refuse to bring anything to the table, every bit as guilty of perpetuating this cultural downward spiral of bottomless mass consumption as all the "normies" they condescend to.

still spewing the rush of fuck-yeah-something-like-this… but then reality bricks across that rush. there's no one out there, and even there was, the vision would ultimately become compromised. talked down to by undeservedly arrogant  status obsessives or having to speculate on the minefield headspaces of mercurial loons and habitual liars. i would just as eagerly volunteer my stud-talents for the manual insemination process of a jostled beehive that was recovered from an apiary that had been left in a state of disrepair after a chance encounter with a roving pack of nuclear boars.

I'm just glad to be in a place where all i get is a sporadic light irritation as opposed to paralyzing muscle tension.

dude i know who ate at Jack in the Box found a band-aid at the bottom of his iced tea,  so their happy meal prizes are pretty metal.

maybe I'm just indulging my contrarian side, but I've found that women in music are way less socially radioactive than their sausage-packing counterparts.

licked pregnant. stain glass navel fibers napalmed to mung. lapsing detente spree-stalks the flood glow. hayseed diaphragms will crisp in the spill. bruise gradients. slivering grip fondles engorged carotids. palm gloves fashioned with suckers like the tentacles of a squid. tugs the back of my scalp. the viscous foam of their salivary glands relieves my dehydration. proceeding lobs are smeared into a gossamer mask that is to be dried, peeled, eaten, and swallowed. the tunneling hush of a gasping whore blades the root a pout has clutched, the tubular drone of flushing mists at the flash of their wound-tight clenching.

bliss consortium. walled up cunts hold council with my seething. they inquire of its origin, and i delight in my failure to elaborate. i just want my head to be their fuck-murder set piece... to vacuum phantom ejaculate with the full heft of my lungs... for bone, brain, and cock to core themselves into their curated void... for organic spackle to blot out the stars of this private universe.

Indonesian haze. toasted rust annuls the scald. prostate-play with a glass-eye. ulcerated clustering thrush crawls the walk in sofa-skin hoods. free hugs from an active suicide bomber. muscle-wolves bless the fade-outs for picking up my trash.

mascara goats. panga thresher inspects for pebbles. marbling oculus drops the gut-braid. serial numbers compartmentalize depressive episodes. ground of stalks in tea-stained humus, lobbing back-worn tentacled gags. butt plugs bejeweled with a bulk of spring-loaded googly-eyes so it looks like clowns are crawling out of your asshole. just because i am not following you doesn't mean that you are not being followed.

splenetic release of crashing tensions. i seem to exist only in states of reality that are anxious gradients of pure frustration. this desperation so thick it humidifies the air around me. a reoccurring fantasy of having my cock and balls pushed through a hole in a plank of plywood, pints of blood being drawn toward it by gloved fingers, tied down with velvet ropes, hacked to pieces with Ugandan machetes, the wound stuffed with gauze and cauterized into a black market trans-op vaginal cavity, toasted to the color of rust. the stew-meat remains of my cock dried to a lambskin jerky, rolled over a strap-on like a condom full of hog gristle, to be worn by the first woman who ever taught me what it was to process a broken heart, and fucked back up the hole it left behind, lubricated in the residue of its gash.

even the most immediate and accessible degrees of beauty seem avoidant to my grasp.

the mediocrities once settled for in a pinch have been removed from the open options by ever-tilting sexual political customs and perpetually ramping technological access to higher rungs of the social ladder. nothing to do but simmer within a private multiverse... its guidebook increasingly fogged by unwashed cum.

- from *Laconique* by Simone Vanique (translated from French by Ghislaine Nudesco for Villation Books)

grin alone. snuff film needle drop. cut fuckers menstruate fire ants. due to these new laws prohibiting single men at movie screenings, it looks like the missing cheerleader i keep locked up in the shed with the purloined mannequin legs will be getting some air.

incompetent white female. garbage fire shit show. underground cellars floored with beachhead. obstinate displays of paranoid anger in the public sphere usually indicate voracious searches of decorum-cratering pleasures in the hermetic chamber. ever see a pig that could spit-roast you?

pink sweat. denim and dishwater bubbling dura mater. your indifference is a labyrinthine gorge. clothespin kidney stone. this is not the ideal medium for actualizing these passions. i'd prefer them in a form less cryptically sensate and more authoritatively corporeal. organs humidified by the breath of an opening. follicles crackling in a wind around the knuckles. not just these frustrated words bound to struggle in capturing the severity of the idea.

rent-free grow sore. defecate liquid to soothe their throats. cooling heads with red t-shirts that have been thoroughly soaked in deep evening panic urine. handcuffed to the steering wheel of a pedophile's rolling butcher shop; a white van that's been stripped down to the frame and left stranded on active railroad tracks.

I'm grateful for women who are ill at ease with ventilated emotions that aren't some variant of wearyingly vindictive paranoid hostility. civilization will not shift course from oblivion without ceaselessly unthinking brutality. the universe is the brain of creation and mankind are the derangement indicators blotting the grey matter on its cat-scan.

amplification spiral. i'm a stroker. i'm a choker. i'm a blackface joker. boiled autumn. jumping rope with chicken parts. spurts emerge in the traffic's piss. cadence quakes goose the fore-bone. lucid dream techniques applied to blood sugar levels. the person who is sick of having creepy baby imagery shoved in their face is me.

it almost seems as if many in my local "fetish community" use BDSM as a way *out* of fucking... and their gift for spin has made those who seek a release-chaser after extreme foreplay feel as if they are inauthentic... that they are somehow on some "higher level" than those who wish to cap off a session of intensity-ratcheting paces with a soul-excoriating screw.

vulval stalactites. ballast discharge. sweat halts the calm. plume of regurgitate suspended beneath chest. groaning excrement simmers through a rogue network of stifling cavities. crippled by a rushing want to articulate the brain attack's surprise.

Switch Rigger. Sadist Degrader. Primal Brat. Experimental Non-monogamist. Masochist Rope bunny. Primal Voyeur. deeply frustrated by lacking reciprocation but reluctant to open others up to the reality of this anxiousness because piss-shouting MRAs have monopolized hetero angst and turned it into a malignant sociopolitical ideology. Dominant Degradee. Submissive Exhibitionist. Slave Daddy. Mistress Owner. Pet Boy. Vanilla Ageplayer. pirouette with steak knives through the ruins of a shopping mall?

red light offense. strategic gapes. dopamine surf. severed head sex jelly. the sole instance of female attention in my day-to-day proclivities are among the playact-enthused avatars of the more telegenic examples of random societal debris,; their predetermined affections as reciprocal as a power struggle between a couch potato and a cathode ray.

in the last three years i've been sharply dressed

down with barely concealed prejudicial hostility for reasons that oscillate between the roughly valid and the emotionally misaligned. the common thread between these articulated baby-shakings has been the overriding instinct across all the ideological spectrums to unforgivingly pummel anyone with a whiff of opposition to their micro-specific agendas into unconditional surrender or, failing that, existence scrubbing exile.

I've inadvertently alienated friends and family because i lack the tools one needs to feign politeness when they reveal their emphatic devotion to studiously ghoulish over killers who would only urinate to extinguish the flames of a burning pediatric hospital if their bladders were loaded with kerosene. because the thought of otherwise decent people being enthralled to the point of faculty-debilitating mania with these excretea-glowering choad-spores... even when their malignant loathsomeness is held to be self-evident...has driven me to a state of being where the only diet of input that keeps me regular... that comforts the compacted junkyard dunes in my content-battered cranium... would be a steady stream of meticulously investigated true sex crime ASMR dialogues.

that's how frustratingly unproductive i find my occasionally renewed attempts at navigating the landmine marathon of interpersonal connection to be in these wit-excoriating hard red days, where even the most cadaverously irredeemable are in lopsided possession of a cosmo-numerical supply of tireless advocates, a self-replicating shock load of legalese dadaists who would spontaneously combust into a perma-expanding burst of molecular unicorn sparkles before condescending to waver in their contrarian obstinance, sneering belligerence, "alternative" fortitude, and creakily undergirded resistance-favoring arguments... all pointedly targeted at naked-faced reality.

- from *Laconique* by Simone Vanique (translated from French by Ghislaine Nudesco for Villation Books)

florescent monochrome. a length of string knotted through the pull tab hole of a slider body. under flesh quakes from stifled frenzy. vaginal scarab giving birth to calcified octuplets through an infected urinary tract. mill hooker rug burn abrades the cut-up bitch, boiled to a pose like making a sandwich in the shower with their mouth. a concrete shank of throbbing blood, the slit of its edge pearled with a bead; a glass cutter wick crowning the tack-gash.

a resin-brained geriatric fuck-clown is continually forgiven and rewarded after an unbroken lifelong pattern of cocking up everyone and everything in his immediate orbit. the hard rock dad hero worship of That 70s Junkie Fashion Cadaver. mind-fuckery vomit art from the fetid mind of nobody who remains still in the calm of a pillow fight with cinderblocks at Gymboree. easily susceptible to becoming overwhelmed by the venereal urge to punt these caterwauling toe heads square into the churning mouth of an active cement mixer. never with deliberate intent have my routine frustrations been positioned to mirror the stubborn loops of radicalized misogynists and inevitable gunmen. the patterns of my interior are stubbornly resistant to such corporeal actualizations.

angrily bewildered. cellar climate for a month's span. rubber chicken fingers drown in bright yellow honey mustard, less for the flavor than for the moisture. the pattern of the stocking's top band vaguely suggest piled human remains that have been arranged in a trench by libidinal Neanderthals; green carnivores that mine plaster dick-rot in the faith that phones will carry them. entelodont laughing place fucked until the paintings breathe. forever knocked back to zero.

selective rejecter. decadent overseer. the clipped vernacular of a curated fringe. knee scab tarpit. wet nightmare pantheon. tomb whore profile traced by light of paper doll garden snakes. junk thought block surge. blight like a plume. brick teeth clot the featured bursts of looking mercury. skeleton present. cringe mythos. i wrote this song after you hit a tree. carnival succubae brush the fanning spermatozoa. your father didn't die; he escaped.

cold Florida. gymnasium glory hole auctioneer. jizz resined garbage brains stoke mongoloid displays of self-nullifying idiot cruelty. comb through a folder on my hard drive containing over five years' worth of unrealized music projects until i can taste the contents of a thermometer. the mixed frustrations of unrealized creativity, a sudden barrage-raid on my finances, years of sexual inactivity, my favorite season being woefully abbreviated, and a continued lack of reciprocation on this (and other) platforms has left me in a state of fatalistic anxiety that seems to have no desistance on the immediate horizon.

*KIRITSIS revisits his two favorite episodes from Daxis' Chickens on Trampolines compilation: "CHICKEN BRAINS" and "CHICKEN RIBS".*

*KIRITSIS was rejected from a literary anthology about snuff films because his work was described as being "too much like watching footage from a slaughterhouse", which is somehow both insulting and complimentary.*

*KIRITSIS obtains sexual arousal under the false pretenses of being handicapped.*

*KIRITSIS views anything outside of his exponentially narrowing micro verse of anally curated specificities with an impenetrable smattering of passive aggressive contempt.*

*KIRITSIS keeps his bondage gear in a diaper bag.*

*KIRITSIS hopes he'll live to witness the ascent of a sexually liberated globe-trotting First Lady, not the assembly line succession of interchangeable home shopping networkers or the made-to-order real dolls fresh off the white slave pageant circuit.*

*KIRITSIS believes himself to be the basis for "Fidelio": the mad arch-criminal killer in Griselda Scapelli's sole directorial effort;* THE WHIP SAW *(released stateside under the title* SURREAL KILLER; *a name the media dubbed KIRITSIS after word spread of his aktions). "Fidelio", portrayed by the reliably vicious character actor Benito Sarignazzi, bears no small resemblance in both appearance and temperament to KIRITSIS, though Scapelli herself claims the intention was to pay homage to Umberto Lenzi's movie adapatation of the* KRIMINAL *fumetti.*

*when he was in high school, KIRITSIS was the front man for a prank black metal band named ESQUILAX, who he formed with members of his short-lived metallic hardcore band SWORN VIRGIN (principals of which would go on to play in CONNIOSUMER), whose backstory was that they were members of the Norwegian Black Circle who were hiding out on Long Island, but couldn't resist the pull of underground black metal, and decided to bring the genre to the suburbs of New York by forming their own band. the jig was up for ESQUILAX after someone pointed out that their name was derived from a gag on* the Simpsons.

*KIRITSIS refuses to eat pastas that are flat and smooth because it feels to him like eating a bowl of live wriggling eels.*

veal cuts drizzling film grain. marinate your pig as it raves through a snarl. cowbell glaucoma. puberty meat breath. letter bomb diaphragm goat-scream "smegma ferret" within the fish market waft of an idol grinder's reek. were i to be assuredly depleted of all remaining scruples, i could envision a scenario where i activate a gloom-riding nostalgia hollow that had be slothfully christened with a sub-inspired nomenclature along the powdered cadaver veins of "Morbid Immolation" or "Broken Cannibal" or "Malevolent Angel Carnage".

boiling October into freezing November. the dissociative rapport of a reality contortionist. slurried reams of lice encode the grievance-spore. attempts at interaction have me feeling as if i were caged beneath the kill floor of a slaughterhouse where the grating is paved over by the minute with a pooling intestinal pour. the jailers find me suspended by gelatinous wings of pulled out lung, strobing against the abyssal caverns of incidental void.

frustrated. frustrating. frustration. frustrate. slipping

in and out of depressive episodes. worn from stifling stalker inclinations. hollow validation of inadvertent resilience. where's the reciprocation? do i worship her like a god or fuck her like a pig? site crashes again, triggering another round of ballistic obscenities muted to a hush that are no less the throat-shredders of a full volume paint-eroding scream. oscillating pangs of naive violation. knife in my teeth pulled to hollow behind the tonsils. trying to open up about my fixations in these caustically sex-negative time feels like trying to aim your masturbation into a tree shredder.

lamps of holed bone. tapping stones worm-line their night glass.

*KIRITSIS snorts crushed Ambien that's been served on a panty shield with a reptilian wag and a pulse-beat claw, nylons worn like a sackcloth hooding the victim of a lynch mob, road flare technicolor spiking the gels of his skeleton's gleam.*

junkyard Baphomet child oven. cut-up no-wave sub-opera lovingly restored by deviance curators. urban grime-goth in a doom-metallic splatter of malarial neon slime. synesthetic god-terror from the cruelty-molded beauty of rupturing hermeticism. funereal art-gore from the mind's tactile scum chamber. getting kicked really hard in the nuts over and over while a courtroom full of attractive muckbangers point and laugh and your stupid & useless swollen organ.

basement-aged spite in a hypno-swirl of mid-tempo hardcore drag. between the murder-y cynicism and the abattoir vomit trough emerges this weaponized excreta pile. the kaleidoscopic punishment of a heart-of-carnage universe blisses out in a lysergic revelry.

continually awakens feeling consumed. xacto knives breaded with a mealy feed that drops from the gullets of maternal sparrows.

*KIRITSIS has come to believe that the only viable option for relieving the wearied zeitgeist of this debilitating ennui... which for his part has shaved down his once considerable empathy to an icepick-sharp pitilessness.. is somehow a particular 43% of all Americans were compelled by horsewhip and firehoses of chucky diarrhea to march single-cunting-file in a vertically daisy-chained tower of rusted meat grinders, their pureed pour culminating in a blister-glowing orange moat of boiled-to-lava heavy metals.*

*KIRITSIS knows that in order the achieve this specific goal he will require no garment less than the Ceremonial Dermis of A M R U; a full body stocking whose mythology indicates having been stitched together from the skin fragments of the earliest bipedal tribes of the earth, shedding's which have been scrimshawed with incantations and later pasted with parchments relevant to each generational inheritor since the time of the First Worshipped. the name "A M R U" comes from the only letters on the pelt that are recognizable to modern eyes.*

*the C.D.A. is believed to have been seamed by the mates of the ELEMPATH who constructed CLOROPHRAGM; the elemental Brobdingnagian who avenged the collateral victims of the long war between the NOSANGUINES and the GORGRES by obliterating all but the scantest of their ranks. the purpose of the C.D.A. was for its wearer to obtain the accumulated essences of all the extinct tribes of the earth. an unforeseen side effect of wearing the C.D.A. was what would come to be referred to as "the Shock Load"; an sensory overdose that would often drive the wearer into states of severe confusion and bewildered aggression.*

*the C.D.A. would find itself slipping over the figures of some of the most influential and dangerous individuals in history, but none whose loathsomeness would prove to be as long lastingly impactful as the first GUIGNOL; the sinister terrorist who emerged at the tail-end of the 19th century to spread a malignant corporeal mantra of time-deepening carnage through senselessly ornate campaigns of physical annihilation and deeply deranged ravings in both print and radio. when the first GUIGNOL disappeared, the C.D.A. was considered to be lost with him, and the subsequent inheritors of the Golgothian Ghoul's lethal legacy would be forced to approximate its aesthetic, the look growing further and further removed from the original shroud.*

**{VOID}**

*KIRITSIS understands that only the true C.D.A. will suffice... that any attempts to counterfeit its imagery will be treated as little more than a glorified cosplay... but since any chance if its recovery is ever remote, he is resigning himself to the fact that this malarial indifference crippling the population will proceed unabated, until the core narrows to a straight razor, splitting the blood of the world down to the corpuscles.*

frozen squid bullets. id-smacked corpulence gliding spongy frames... redeemed in the bleeds choleric mutants fanged. liver spots crackle on the x-ray, as if the brain had been swirling in a tumbler full of Clorox. scabs across the knuckles resemble tiny eyelids hued an irritant pink from untreated rings of petrified conjunctivitis. the first lady's alright if you masturbate to skin grafts.

*as he has done when inclined to enter the mock-snuff realities of the whispered internets, where he often materializes as a hypnagogic wraith of flickering binary code, KIRITSIS astral projects his leering ectoplasmic essence into a large circular room that resembles the bay port of a pulp villain's deep space headquarters. papering the circumference of the wall is an unspooled mural; a micro-detailed acrylic depiction of a swirling galaxy comprised of blood, guts, gore, and bones; stars of teeth, moons shaped like skulls, corpuscles in an asteroid belt, planets of brains ringed with offal, arterial cosmic detritus revolving around an eyeball sun.*

*there is a throne in the east corner of the room. a woman is slumped in the seat, right leg draped over the arm of the throne. she has been poured inside a violet catsuit, sleeveless so she can display the meticulously carved sinew of her strong arms. the neckline of the rubbered body sheath has been cut to resemble the silhouette of an octopus, cleavage beading against a cephalopod window. her silver hair frames her face in a hood of wild frizz, a face whose eyes are hidden behind a pair of mirrored sunglasses... the kind worn by motorcycle cops... and whose mouth is covered by what looks to be a SARS mask quilted from barcodes.*

*she has unzipped the crotch of her catsuit, letting her meaty cunt breathe. spreading the bloated labial maw, lips that look to have been caught between a car door and pulled, her vaginal cavity is visibly lined with weeping suction cups, which adhere themselves to the palm-gloved fingers as she brands the venereal foam across the protrusive knuckles.*

*in the center of the room there is a triple-wide dissecting table on a rotating scissor trestle. a stocky woman, body covered in long textured birthmarks, is on her knees, spinning her drool around the width of a vascular strap-on that appears to be leathered in pulled white jerky. laying down in front of her is what could only be described as a living meat doll; thirstily squirming and vacuumed tight inside a patchwork skin coat that has been tattooed and scarified with images and texts whose arcane origins have long since been abandoned by the bullet-train-borings of time. only four letters are recognizable among any known alphabets; A, M, R, and U.*

*an unanticipated surge of percussive mental energy blast-fades KIRITSIS back to his room before his glitching spectral form can bear witness to the climatic epiphany of this multi-versal shock load, where he resumes his regretful corporeal stasis with a disappointment that verges on apocalyptic pessimism.*

peak inoculation. pessimist sermonizing obliviously adroit. a clockwork plumage of obstinate scabs blossoms from the gullet projectiles of terminally aggrieved hayseeds who menstruate cringe from syphilitic lunchmeat grey matter.

*KIRITSIS considers himself the world's foremost authority on THE GLOOM. THE GLOOM is the title character in a series of pulp novels in the 1930s; a pre-superhero vigilante in the mold of The Shadow, the Spider, the Black Bat, the Green Hornet, and others.*

*much like the aforementioned, THE GLOOM was depicted as being a lean male clad in a suit, tie, fedora, and gloves. the character's defining feature was a dark blue mask, cinched at the neck with a belt, tight enough to outline the skull beneath the flesh of the head. the slack of the cloth was long enough to drape over his shoulders and back, tatters skirting the floor about the polished feet of THE GLOOM. when launching into attack, THE GLOOM would burst through the slit-divide of this sheer deep sky membrane, choking the life out of his adversaries like a stunned civilian thrusting open their own body bag after having been mistaken for a cadaver.*

*THE GLOOM was created by Silvio Rotpule, who wrote all the novels and painted all the covers, which, like the yellowing text within, had the distinction of being exponentially more lurid and disturbing than the contemporaneous costumed avengers who found membership within the fraternity of this milieu. at times THE GLOOM felt more like a precursor to arch-fiends like Coffin Joe or Sadistik then the heroic (if casually problematic) crime fighters sharing his shelf space.*

*as for Rotpule, he disappeared before the final novel in THE GLOOM series could ever be completed, which was promised to finally reveal the ghoulish guardian's true identity.*

*a little under thirteen years later, THE GLOOM would serve as the inspiration for Jimmy and Livia Monday's superhero THE LIVING GRAVE, which was published by Coal Tiger Comics after the success of the couple's FEAR WOMAN comic. rather than a shawl, THE LIVING GRAVE would wear an actual covering for dead bodies as a cape and cowl, with matching grey shorts, gloves, and boots over chalky blue skin. THE LIVING GRAVE failed to match the popularity of FEAR WOMAN, and was cancelled after three issues. THE LIVING GRAVE was recently resurrected in Mills Moor's FEAR WOMAN relaunch for Cool Ranch Comics, this time as a jilted adversary for the title character... an arch which falls in line for Moor's penchant for insider meta-commentary.*

*another connection to both THE GLOOM and THE LIVING GRAVE can also be drawn from the Italian Exploitation film industry. when giallo enfant terrible Vincenzo Scapelli took a work-for-hire gig as the writer / director of a blatant Pet Cemetery knock off, he chose to name the film LIVING GRAVES as an homage to the Mondays' "lesser" creation (Scapelli drew heavily from the couple's FEAR WOMAN strips for his softcore anti-heroine film series FUMETTA, so this comes as no surprise).*

*Scapelli's LIVING GRAVES was produced during what some see as a low point for the auteur, a cycle which included Great Value versions of Alien, Predator, Terminator, Road Warrior, and Conan the Barbarian (COSMUTANT, SCORCH POACHER, MECHROBORG, PAVEMENT MAIDEN, and VULTERICK: BASTARD WRAITH OF GOZ respectively), as well as the underseen but over vilified SOV "scat-roughie"* MERDA RAGAZZA, *which played like a grimy compilation of characters and ideas from the works of Boyd Gintload (most specifically* MONDO GONZO, *the cat-and-mouse thriller that pitted Eurosleeze icon Astrid Melora against Blacksploitation heroine Rhea Uhua). these were hatchet jobs that seemed beneath the director of the classic* HEADGEAR. *with the benefit of hindsight, many cinephiles have suggested Scapelli did these films as a kind of "fuck you" to an industry and fan base who rejected some of his more "high concept" ideas; namely* IMPALE HER; *his X-rated arthouse take on* Dracula; *, while emphatically embracing projects he deemed inferior, such as* Sow, *his biggest hit to date but an flagrant bid for the American slasher market that Scapelli himself has called "culturally malignant".*

*this period in Scapelli's filmography is particularly careless, mean-spirited, and wearing its bald-faced cynicism on its sleeve... but it's nonetheless an interesting psychological study of an artist tangled in the throes of raw torment. the viewers of these lumberingly grotesque reams of shameless cinematic opportunism are in fact bearing witness to a creative processing his inhospitable emotions through the only medium available to him at the time. Scapelli found a lot of parallels to his headspace in the overall themes of the story* LIVING GRAVES *was shamelessly purloining, and he has since claimed that this is the film that reenergized him after years of setbacks and disappointments.*

*the plot of* LIVING GRAVES *does indeed stick close to* Pet Cemetery; *in a rural community there is a graveyard that is believed to have restorative properties to any who are buried in its ground.* LIVING GRAVES *differs in that the word of this grave has reached beyond the small population of this rural community, and now there is an influx of bereaved who are seeking to bury their loved ones in this graveyard. this is a boom for the town's economy, but too much stress for the ground to bear, and the loved ones start returning with an inflection old timers referred to as "the Gloom" (heh), which is described as the accumulated essences of unnamed eldritch monstrosities who once claimed the grounds as their home. here the film becomes something closer to Lucio Fulci's* the Beyond *or Umberto Lenzi's* Nightmare City, *with the loved ones returning as snarling-ly cannibalistic ghouls who have intermingled vengeful rage with frustrated lust, who proceed to rape and murder anyone and everyone, dragging their victims to the overworked graveyard so their ranks can swell and engulf the world.*

*though* LIVING GRAVES *was Scapelli's strongest film, both conceptually and visually, since* HEADGEAR, *it's also his most demonstrably controversial, as many of the scenes suggested (if not outright declared) bestiality and pedophilia; a claim Scapelli and the film's defenders dispute by saying that these characters were now "something beyond animal or human... something morosely other... ". the film is also notable for its soundtrack, which is highlighted by sleazy arena metal act Chastity Pariah, who perform the pornographically anthemic title song.*

*as for THE GLOOM, the character had a brief but interesting foray into the 1980s comic book market with a mini-series published by ARCHETYPE, written by crime story deconstructionist CHAUNCY HARKIN and drawn with painterly hypnagogic menace by KIEV LIENSBITCZ. later in the 1990s, HECTOR BELLONE's frustratingly restrained movie adaptation of THE GLOOM had the unfortunate luck of opening against STANLEY VERTREFFN's cinematic take on COOL RANCH COMICS anti-hero HORROR SHOW; a character who proved to be riding such a wave of white-hot popularity that a pre-WWII pulp magazine property couldn't even entertain the notion of outmatching its box office muscle. reviews for THE GLOOM film were tepid at best, with critics reserving their harshest comments for the film's star WALLACE BLIND, who phoned in an especially smarmy performance (even for him). contemporary audiences know BLIND better from his extended stay on the sketch comedy program CIRCULAR FIRING SQUAD, where he stinks up the set with an obnoxiously lazy impression of PRESIDENT DAX SPAMIN.*

*ironically, a more serviceable film adaptation of* THE GLOOM *arrived in an unofficial capacity a few years earlier from* RAMSEY SAMUELS, *the underground splatter auteur behind the video store sensation* ROT PRINTS, *who used his first entry into mainstream cinema to craft* BANDAGE PHANTOM: *a kinetically operatic ode to the pulp novel anti-hero, the name of the title character being slightly derived from the second* GLOOM *novel "the Bondage Phantom", where THE GLOOM was for the first time pitted against the villain who would go on to become his arch-enemy; the "dark voodoo priest doctor"* ADEBISI SANGHOULNO.

BANDAGE PHANTOM *would briefly become something of a micro-sensation, with tie-ins that included comic books, a series of novels, a less-than-stellar video game, even more substandard DTV sequels (which saw no creative involvement from* RASMEY SAMUELS), *a TV pilot that was never picked up, some model kits, and an action figure as part of the inaugural set of the* COOL RANCH COLLECTIBLES CINEMA PSYCHOS *toy line, which included* GREASETRAP *from the* SOW *franchise and* HANG NAILS *from the* HIDING IN SANITY *franchise.*

monopolizing hostilities. a towering vehicular pile-up confined to a cloudy bio-dome that's gradually being filled with molasses-thick excreta and urine that possesses the consistency of honey... honey which is

hardening into an amber gum at the sprout...
browning tears streaking the face of a plastic teddy
bear.

*KIRITSIS often exhaustively dwells on speculating
whether or not there are people out there who hate
him as much as he hates others... with that bone-deep
venom normals reserve for dog fight promoters and
baby rapers (unrepentant or otherwise).*

*KIRITSIS likes to reopen the wounds of memory by
imagining conversations between those who have
earned the slavish devotion of his unyielding spite,
where they bond in uneasy laughter over their elite-
tier alumni status among the holo-caustal blacklist of
ruined acquaintances.*

*KIRITSIS ponders the endgame of this reoccurring
mission; becoming a socially malignant asshole of
Anti-God-Level proportions who rapidly loses
everything he cut throats to obtain, glacially expiring
in the jaundiced light of vituperative cosmic isolation.*

Clorox eye drops. cop spit daiquiri. the gnawing lure
of a fuming revolve.

autopsy keepsakes. rot-foam in the ash-chest
consumes the staged repose with a braiding squirm.
idling cancellations stand clear in palsy gaits,
validating the genres their hated once claimed.

burned knuckles on the toaster oven. it has been pink

for a month's time. let this be the last ten years of you. kill your local cool guy.

woman on a branch drops umbrellas from the tree, which pop into blood when landing on the marble cherubs beneath her; glaring's lucid in the splash.

- from *Laconique* by Simone Vanique (translated from French by Ghislaine Nudesco for Villation Books)

12/31/1999; spending New Year's Eve in front of the TV, ditched by "friends" for a party where i'm told i'm not welcome due to having beef with the hosts. since this information was relayed to me by an exhausted target of my restless infatuation, i suspect her of fabricating drama... suggesting the potential for a hospital visit after the host arranges of coalition of those sympathetic to his ends of our feud and sicks them upon me... for want to have an evening of guilt-free fucktime with her most recent paramour, without the inevitable wet-brained brooding of the overweening blood pile who can't take "why are you doing this?" for an answer.

processing a broken heart and coping with abandonment as only an alienated teenager living on Long Island in the late 90s knows how; blasting death metal CDs and hoping that the apocalyptic prophecies of Y2K will not be yet another personally crippling disappointment in a year typified by them.

Flint Rupture's latest music is pretty fucking boring, the *Pubescent Toxic Hippo Ronin* relaunch has everyone contagiously apoplectic over a shitty movie about toys, kids are getting mowed down by automatic weapons during school hours, and everyone makes me feel alone.

12/31/2019; still unpacking thoughts on *CRISIS ACTOR;* Stanley Vertreffn's auteur-driven "New Hollywood" style reimagining of the Agent Paragon villain, starring Ric Gaze as "Rubin Bartleby", a socially isolated mail sorter at a right wing tabloid with dreams of becoming a talking head on hard conservative broadcasts, slowly going mad and eventually donning the guise of the Crisis Actor. finally settled on the conclusion of it being a movie i would've dreamed of at age twenty, when i used to spend a chunk of my time brainstorming ways to synergize a childhood love of superhero comics with my post-adolescent devotions to cult cinema, obscure horror movies, violent arthouse films, sketchy urban legends, serial killer lore, and "ironic" needle drops (good use of "Masquerade" by Berlin).

and yet with *CRISIS ACTOR* being a near-perfect encapsulation of all my life's grease pit obsessions being hailed as zeitgeist-redefining cultural touchstone (though seemingly only because those themes have been trojan-horsed inside a lucrative intellectual property with major studio funding), i feel less validated than ever... my own creative ventures struggling to break even into the most remote margins of relevant discourse.

Flint Rupture's latest music is pretty fucking boring, the *Pubescent Toxic Hippo Ronin* relaunch has everyone contagiously apoplectic over a shitty movie about toys, kids are getting mowed down by automatic weapons during school hours, and everyone makes me feel alone. i can access ass-eating clips on my phone.

prank mace. raw carnage. tumbling growths dimple the blood their udders wept amniotic-pink. a cankered mash bejeweling vomit in the colon's maw. shock trooper midwives brandish copper-peels where lacerations grieve.

fell of hurm. nitrate colonic. savoring the crumbs of child martyr brigades. ironic satire deformed into a nihilistic tirade. i read a textbook this morning and wrote a boring song about it. my words are very intelligent because i heard a philosophy.

corpulent entrails. sniffing panties recovered from a trash can belonging to a fifteen year old with an eating disorder behind the bushes under their bedroom window while they use their favorite childhood toys as masturbation aids with their father's breath moistening the door.

*KIRITSIS takes so much satisfaction in the idea of baby rapers being murdered that he by extension practically welcomes the brutal violation of children so that he can indulge his vicious bloodlust in a situational context to which few will object; revenge-motivated mob justice that will only lead to more broken bodies and shattered minds. it is only in this belief that KIRITSIS feels a connection with the impotent passengers of life who have never lost anything yet still feel that their existence is indispensable.*

Boomer O'Reilly. hawk word sigils marinated scenarios until their flavors overwhelm the drawn dirt. loathing nourishment, wounds in a sheet midwife the pork eggs. i hope ticks explode your urethra. viral forecasts give up the goad. hang in the air like trained threats of a beating. hardware ooze fucked sands inspected for pebbles. the best of you dropped dead before hitting thirty. don't cry. don't raise your eye. it's only child pornography.

*the last time KIRITSIS went to Rubherd Sandwiches, he had their Reuben and it tasted like a wool sock that had been left to soak in a pothole full of melted dirty snow.*

only one tooth bleeds. it's the width of four huddled molars and it grows separate from the others; at the right-hand-most corner of the floor of the mouth.

*when KIRITSIS was in his young twenties, his anger would rise to the category of volcanic for reasons that oscillated from bafflingly pedantic to comically fabricated. a significant instance of such an scorched-earth flare up occurred when KIRITSIS, in a scarce instance of good fortune, had somehow managed to become involved with PIXY DEVILLE; a fetish-centric pin-up / burlesque performer (with a concentration on belly-dancing) of more than scant recognition, who to this day remains a reliable draw at TATTERDEMALION.*

*the two found a sudden libidinal repoire with one another, and proceeded to engage in what would no doubt be the pinnacle of KIRITSIS' sexual backstory. however... and there is usually a however... PIXY DEVILLE had something of an overweening fascination with men and women who were part of "the 27 Club"; rockstars and celebrities who had passed away by age twenty-seven.*

*for reasons whose rationale seemed in his mind to be valid, this particular obsession had cratered the patience of KIRITSIS, and he launched into a heated tirade, laced with ballistic expletives and dripping with bile and smarm, about "well connected narcissists and overvalued junkies being wrongfully deified upon their premature death". the pre-scribed "shock" of these events of ceased mortality were illusive to KIRITSIS, as such outcomes had all but been prophetic, if not solidified; the projective behavior of these carelessly mythologized action figures being a preamble for self-annihilation.*

*when PIXY DEVILLE simply laughed off the emotionally misaligned ramble, this caused KIRITSIS to vibra-mire in his boiling plasmatic kurd, his perspiration drip manifesting as a vaporous gel, reddish-blue steam roiling out from honeycombed pores.*

*it is often observed that the number one fear of men is that women will laugh at them, and the number one fear of women is that men will kill them.*

*wanting to make his point perfectly clear, but also not wanting to derail the bone-train, KIRITSIS decided to split the difference. he noticed that PIXY DEVILLE had a red sharpie marker tucked behind her ear. with a quick motion, KIRITSIS snatched the marker. KIRITSIS then found a spot on the wall of PIXY DEVILLE's bedroom that wasn't covered with a poster or a magazine page, and punched a shallow hole into it. then, with the sharpie, KIRITSIS proceeded to write a message directed at PIXY DEVILLE across the damage. it was simply two words:*

## *YOUR HEAD.*

ACRIMIRE (GRISTLE ICARUS). cement scabies. sucked in and down from the rib to its paper. caught in wet clay. the body indents in the wake of its peel. steep imprint of a fuck-towel's mold. their shadow pumped to a crime-scene weight. orbiting coffins. gossamer lava. verging on the edge of combustible ugly. a spine of clothespins. bat soup candle pour. lashed until the produce crowns.

gesticulating chum-sacks leak giblets from the cork's impact. the buzz saw grates with the structure of a pop. shadow-flesh neath the fraying crotch. gridded hooves wore the art film grain. standing bones like the whispered pikes that grow bulbed from their voided eyes.

trauma braggart. rubber tongue conveyer belt. baby semen vomit stains. spider abdomens of jointed bone spurs chip lattice into the grumbling pavement. mummified in crinkling jerky, wadded from clusters of geyser-ing abscess, he uses his mouth to pickle the meat of his mutilated cock. counterfeit period irrigates their opera-burns. sweet-talked into feeding it blood.

Sudafed lisp. decaying animal skeletons crocheted from string lodged inside the collective head until it makes me cum. foam leprosy. acquiesce to your cruelest worm. tangled cables grin. breaking teeth on the lick. red veal concentrate in narrowing enemas speckled the glory-holed coffins.

"i would've used the President Spamin speech as toilet paper were the pages not already covered in shit."

- Whillice Rison, from the *SpaminKiller* newsletter.

*if KIRITSIS wants to vent his considerable frustrations about the current administration and they wind up within earshot of one of these smarmy contrarian jizz-maps who needs to remark with some above-the-fray-cool-dude garbage about the previous president "being equally bad", then KIRITSIS is going to kindly suggest that that they take their faux-nihilistic mediocrity the fuck out of his face, or theirs just might end up a gimp mask being worn by him while he rapes the severed heads of their bloated whore mothers.*

blood & bullshit. mechanic-stains where the cottoned mound rides. tensions rope their dreading skulls. loaded nerves have braided the nails to navigate this orbit of clots.

zinematone. ambient vulgarity. forked orchid. mushroom cumulus. chicken scratch face tattoos. concave pregnancy camouflaging thumbtacks where its Capgras teemed. glass bottle shoved up the cunt is to be smashed with a ball peen hammer. an over-compiled dossier of burdensome entitlements. ruin verge. stands on shoulders. folded breast meat in the shape of a wallet. concrete beehive. Rose McGowan enables and emboldens child pornographers.

*KIRITSIS possesses equal reactive capacities of neurotic sputtering and vindictive eloquence.*

*KIRITSIS dumpster-dives for used condoms so he can load syringes with the jism left in their reservoirs and inject the cum up the cunts of lauded debutantes who passed out at pretentious rooftop dance parties.*

*years of excessive internet exposure have rendered KIRITSIS a petty, ridiculous, retarded infant who expects everyone in his orbit to be on the exact same page as him about all things. he hasn't done his best to sequester his own bitchy hot takes and contrarian smarm within the walls of his own social media accounts.*

Nosferwaifu. shoulder lotioned in the midst of a sneeze. message board anecdotes in corporeal form. mortuary merkin. cosmic horror porn grows into the baby tongue. grunting sweat-drip tore the blinking snout a curdling tuber sludged to the floor-bed. cancer-scare urgency undergirds their rapes. medicine bottle resin in the spice of a fleck. let's not turn this back page orgy into breaking news of an active shooting.

injuries become clear. throat burned. face covered in bruises and cuts. eyes blackened. abrasions on top of feet. teeth knocked out. incision above penis. ligature marks on ankles. cigarette burns all over body. a skull fracture. BB gun pellets lodged in lung and groin. Not content with murdering child, forcing to endure countless beatings, sleep in cupboard at foot of bed, handcuffed to door, mouth gagged and face covered. eat nothing but cat litter.

gastric masochism. fitted for a smarm piece. cherry

chocolate chowder fills the shoes of a mailbox. the drying sexual mucus of an impromptu cannibal wraps the itch around a driveway block, subsuming a millennia for a name to reach their throats.

two men visit father of son and daughter. stress of visit puts father in hospital. father is on a gurney. son and daughter are beside the father. two bigger men visit father and son and daughter in hospital. the two bigger men point large silver handguns at father on the gurney. the two bigger men are inches away from the head of the son. stress of visit puts father outside of hospital room window. son is at vending machine on level below father's hospital room. son watches from window as father plummets to the ground of the hospital's garden. daughter is walking in the hospital's garden with a boy she met in the hallway. father hits the ground a few feet ahead of them. father bursts like a practice dummy made out of pinata confetti and filled with ketchup-based chili. daughter runs toward father. boy laughs.

- from *Laconique* by Simone Vanique (translated from French by Ghislaine Nudesco for Villation Books)

sleep paralysis hallucination cosplay, seppuku jazzercise. laryngitic aloe. worn as a clown in the mouth of a shark. viral angst. cocaine geodes. lungs

{VOID}

rollout vapor staining the back of teeth. please don't try.

*when consumed by onanistic need, one of the memories KIRITSIS dredges up is the one time with PIXY DEVILLE when she fucked his ass with one of her nipples; which were already long and large, but made larger and longer with a suction device.*

corner of space wallpapered with vertical gym-mats body had earlier been shoved against. figure poured into oil-thin second skin of wet chrome, tinted a shade of violet that comes to be reprised in the swelling patchwork of welts and bruises palms and fists left across torso in the wake of the sporadic attacks brought upon by willfully shaky ability to follow one rule: look forward. fingernails are scraping up and down ribs, gaze remains averted from the micro-tatters of skin protruding from the shallow wounds. breath warming soft parts , the hisses and sighs that spelunk libidinal floodgates, causing all the blood to surge downhill, eyes remained locked on the blue corner of the room. reward this renewed sense of good behavior by occasionally darting into sight, appearing like a shape that emerges between states of sleepiness and alertness... A hypnagogic caregiver.

*KIRITSIS spent the afternoon and early evening reacquainting himself with his comic book collection, focusing almost entirely on random back issues of* WET LOOK: *a "bad girl" series published by*

*AbbaNoir Studios in the mid-late 1990s that arrived at the tail end of that subgenre's heyday.*

WET LOOK *told the story of a young woman named Leena Dial; a popular but controversial talk radio host living in an unnamed city. during the midst of a particularly vicious heatwave (a convenient excuse for every character to be wearing next to nothing but skimpy underwear and a sheen of sweat), Leena is violently attacked by a grotesque gang of deformed street punks. raped and left to bleed out in a sudden burst of soaking rain, Leena collects herself and walks to the bridge, throwing herself off of it so she can drown. instead of sinking to the bottom, Leena is enveloped by a conveniently placed chemical plume, which mutates her genetics, giving her vaguely defined power and strength. when Leena reaches the shore, she finds herself covered in residue from the plume, which drips and dries over just enough portions of her anatomy for her to not be completely naked, creating a low-cut one piece "bathing suit" (really just a thong hiked up over her shoulder that magically curves around the breasts and conceals the nipples), short clawed gloves that don't reach the wrists, and thigh-high spiked heel boots; all shiny and patterned with drips. she slicks her hair back, sliding her fingers across her throat, mouth, and eyes, the trail of the plume-substance leaves weeping cut patterns that gives the impression of Leena's neck and face being vertically slashed. dubbing herself "Wet Look", she embarks on a god mode campaign of gruesome revenge, taking on her attackers first, and then moving up the ranks to their superiors, while encountering other foes and threats along the way and occasionally pausing to lament on her lost life in overwrought monologues that marinate the eyes with affected regret.*

WET LOOK *was fully saturated with the cruder trends of outlaw comics milieu; beautifully actualized full color cover art that belied the haphazard black-and-white interiors, eagerly practiced brooding, club goer ambiance as understood by someone who has yet to leave their bedroom, thorny cityscapes, tortured vampiric romance, a tumbling succession of revenge-motivated story arches, a female protagonist whose body type and facial features held an unwavering dependance on (what was then) the preferred models of mainstream pornography, a mongoloid adolescent's understanding of the consequences of sex and violence, and seemingly every single character being afflicted with intermittent explosive disorder.*

WET LOOK *wasn't a particularly hot title in its time, but it became subject to re-discovery after it was revealed that the book's artist/writer Flynn Ronalds was in fact a teenaged Flint Rupture; created just before he formed the arena industrial act CHANNEL 11, which would eventually lead to a promising film career in the form of HIDING IN SANITY, which gave horror film fans a new ready-made icon in the form of "Hang Nails", the film's villain (a rough draft of the character appears in issue 13 of WET LOOK, the last one of the series).*

priapistic validation. tubes strap upright. leather runs the broken hole. huff the leakage a blistering powdered. evacuate copulation's halo. spurting pink thrush a carotid lunged.

stress atrophy. wrenching muscle-swirl knotted into gurney-binds. slipping into a bath below a ceiling of chainsaws rigged to the twine garroting my throat. peeling heat. bureaucratic slog. curving stains mark off the rings tracing air removed from heads.

psydiarrhetic hemorrhage-scapes. boiled syringe cleans off the fat from jerky masks of grilled Lepus. sex worker pelts contain the scald detritus boned with mites' refuse. erosion fans a test pattern in the blood-side of a cutter's skin. littering guts breathe rubbered palms cloud-scarified in roped orbits.

*KIRITSIS can smell the residual crotch musk in the white fluff of the gelatin-soft back pillow that was utilized in assistance with his masturbation practices two nights before. as something of a oneristic expansion pack, he had drawn up the memory of the time he had fucked the tits of PIXY DEVILLE. this particular recollection was unique. PIXY DEVILLE had wrapped her tits so completely around KIRITSIS' cock that her nipples could kiss each other. KIRITSIS then held this mammary gland ouroboros in place while PIXY DEVILLE took a long piercing needle and pressed it against the side of her right nipple until it came out the side of her left nipple. with the tits now held together, both PIXY DEVILLE and KIRITSIS put their hands behind their heads and proceeded as customary with the act; locking mean eyes and harmonizing their amorous sneers with the rhythm of their piston-paced rubbing.*

media thread anarchist. affluent desperation in brooding obscurity. the clinically depressed backend of a gallows humor geek show.

solitude withdrawal. are you often accused of deadening the room? maybe the real coronavirus were the friends we made along the way.

girth guilt. punctures web the face with burgundy latticework. voyeur secretions of indeterminate ruin. mutilated hooker plank ballast. don't call Italian Electronic Music "Gabbergool".

flapping cleaver. exit scab. a scalp made of chains. suckling bulbous toe knuckle. coral bacteria rung out into pried open eyehole. optic nerves like florescent spirochetes. liquid protein down vitamin deficient gullet. bearing gritted teeth in the sudden throttle. clay tuber snagged in the portal's give. spackle hooks into ridged gash. smoothing to cone in the gossamer bleed. abdominal grid like floors of upturned roaches.

TFW your lifestyle for the past three years is

considered the most extreme response to a global pandemic.

*when KIRITSIS seeks to have his erect cock roped with veins yet to have been discovered, he recalls a time where he had met up with PIXY DEVILLE at TATTERDEMALION backstage after one of her performances. her on-stage partner that evening was VIVIAN GAUNTLEAN; an archetypal encapsulation of female supremacy; hard-bodied and sharp featured with a sneer that alone felt like a deep fuck.*

*after closing, the trio took up residence in one of club's "Masochistian" suites; private rooms where patrons and/or performers could expel the randiness that accumulated over the course of an evening's festivities. KIRITISIS optioned to grant his usual sado-master tendencies a holiday and let the two women expunge their deepest darkest wants upon him.*

*VIVIAN strapped him into swing that hung from the ceiling like a lowered chandelier of belt and chain, locked his ankles in a spreader bar, which she then raised to be situated in a pair of dangling hooks.*

*while VIVIAN positioned KIRITSIS, PIXY DEVILLE ducked into a changing room. when she emerged she was wearing nothing but a thick blue strap-on.*

*VIVIAN then reached for two candles, also blue, and walked toward PIXY DEVILLE , the two trading evil, hungry gazes. VIVIAN circled PIXY DEVILLE thirteen times, each time inching the candles closer to skin. on the thirteenth rotation, VIVIAN halted behind PIXY DEVILLE, raised the candles, and poured the melted wax down her shoulders. PIXY DEVILLE let out a gasp, rendered seductively caustic from excessive marijuana use, as the wax cooled down her tits and formed into a brasserie of oily stalactites. VIVIAN then whispered into PIXY DEVILLE's ear, though it could not be known whether a command was relayed or just a warm spear of breath was shot through the canal.... regardless, PIXY DEVILLE's eyes lit up, followed by a half-open mouth grin that closed her teeth down her bottom lip, dragging it slightly into her mouth.*

*the duo then turned their attention to a hanging KIRITSIS, who strained his neck trying to catch a glimpse of VIVIAN and PIXY DEVILLE, their presence blotted by his squirming prick like a hand trying to block the rays of the sun.*

*"aww Piiiix... look at our fuck-tube over there! they want your cock so fucking bad, don't they?"*

*"huagahh! our fuck-tube certainley does, Viv!"*

*"well? give that needy cunt what it wants, Pix."*

*"yes, Viv."*

*PIXY DEVILLE walked toward KIRITSIS until they*

*were separated only by a hard cylinder of vascular plastic, knocking its head up against his asshole, flicking it like a tongue made rigid by post-mortem stasis.*

*"i'm slipping into this cunt pretty easily, Viv."*

*"i expect nothing less from a walking train-station like them, Pix."*

*at first PIX holds the cock in place, allowing the walls of KIRITSIS's rectum to acclimate the vinyl interloper to its new surroundings. it's not too long before she begins to accelerate her pumping, staring down KIRITSIS with the snarling delight of a determined rapist delaying the throes of their an oncoming orgasm as to further the pain of their assault victim.*

*"Pix; i think this cunt is starting to cry a little."*

*gossamer strands of pre-cum are self-squeezed out of the urethral port, emerging in beaded tears. PIX fucks harder, lowering her chest to KIRITSIS, her face now inches from his. she flicks her tongue at him, which instinctively causes him to do the same.*

*KIRITSIS then feels a hand press down across his windpipe, fingers pinching his carotids just enough to elevate his arousal to a peaking anxiousness. PIX's hands are on his shoulders, so he knows this hand belongs to VIV. soon, his face is being smothered with a glistening asshole, bulbed from seedlings of emerging hair. VIV places her other hand across PIX's throat, raising her head to meet her wide burning eyes.*

*"fuck this cunt with a scream until your whore-cock cums, pig."*

*PIX obliges VIV's request, pounding the tuber into KIRITSIS' ass, overlaying the fuck with sharp grunts that slide through the slivers of her gritted teeth. VIV tightens her grips on both throats, KIRITSIS searching for pockets of air in VIV's saturated holes.*

*without warming, VIV hocks a thick wad of spit onto PIX's face, the saliva dripping down to stain KIRTSIS swollen cock.*

*"make that whore-cock do that, pig. flood the guts of this fuck-tube with your pig-cum."*

*after an abbreviated preamble of hushed curse utterances, PIX collapses her lungs with a paint-peeling howl, which wastes no time instigating a creamed burst from KIRITSIS' prick, dyed bruise-violent from delaying the testicular voiding.*

*"now what, Viv?"*

*"now break your whore-cock off in that pig-cunt."*

*PIX dislodges the strap on from its harness, leaving it to plug up KIRITSIS' asshole. VIV and PIX then undo the straps holding KIRITISIS in the swing, guiding* him down to the floor, where he sits on his knees with his arms phantom-bound behind his back.

"i think this greedy pig knows what's coming, Pix."

"oh yes, my little cocksleeve here knows what's coming... and it ain't him."

PIX wraps her hands across KIRITSIS's throat, raising him up just enough for his dildo-packed ass to hover off the ground.

"now push Daddy's dick out of your slimy cunt."

KIRITSIS complies, his muscles ushering the plastic onto the floor.

"yeah that's it. get all Daddy's cum out of you, too. i want to see my cock marinated in the afterbirth of your miscarriage."

"that's right, Pix; a little cream-of-fetus for our shit-packing princess."

KIRITSIS has remained erect throughout this next phase of the paces.

"eat this cock, dumb-shit."

KIRITSIS chomps his teeth down on the excretea-caked dildo, deep enough to chip off pieces of the toy. he then goes full ravenous; licking and biting and sucking the toy as if it were a chicken leg. VIV and PIX begin to tussle his damp hair and pet his back, *which makes him sink down into the floor, curling up on his side, resting his head on PIXY DEVILLE's lap as she stroked the sides of his face, whispering harsh gratitude's until they droned a hypnotic lull.*

the recall lights the memory fragment as if it were arranged to be photographed by dispassionate professionals when the snap-shot grime of a motel security camera would be a more suitable capture of the psycho-plasmic floating stain.

... wet growths of the quarantine-void... cratering isolation frequency. conducting mass for shut-ins... greasing eye-hole chrome... oral vertigo at the pace of forming blisters... teenagers found mutilated to death by cultists in the bathroom of a public park... obscure eldritch monstrosities bricking in their wounds... renewing a dawn of spiteful insensitivity...

virulent calm. sane gratification decreed non-essential. board the windows, bolt the attic, and load floors with never-ending fear-shits. play killer mask. byzantine lair of excremental salutations curve scimitars heated in the ink vault. generic metaphysical dystopian vigilante revenge fantasies as repetitively inelegant as the idea space of a mass shooter. laconic cognizance. panicked insouciance. it's not "paranoia"; it's "spicy preparedness".

*while KIRITSIS was still on the prowl through the arteries of 5079 Bannon Ave, he found the following piece of writing in the office of VALISE ROTPULE:*

"when the expansion of LUCRASOOKER finally settles, an **A**tonal-harmonious spurt reaching up the arch of various headquarters in the corporate district to down the excrement-crusted **M**aw of the sewage system, it will overwhelm more than half of Fusolk County with blooming gearwork-sores of technological leprosy. the infected will be **R**educed to broken-jointed avatars of the LUCRASOOKER brain-nest; charred remains restructured into funeral home marionettes; **U**nglued skeletons fleshed in a boiling pour of melted black rubber that dried into a gummy paint drip, their janky-motions a wounded-comic response to copper-sparks of phantom stimulations.

"after the area becomes quarantined, those outside its border will give it a new name: MECHROTHAM, which will appear on maps of the island as a psoriatic cluster of tangled livewires, with the enlarged neon-eyed chrome-covered razorback head of LUCRASOOKER rotating at the peak height of MECHROTHAM's "ground-nerve"; the former 5079 Bannon Ave, where NYUNOMARU can be properly incubated to maturity within the walls of the scrap metal yard kaiju."

*hastily translated obscure prophecy or a detailed treatment for a sci-fi monster thriller? regardless, KIRITSIS likes VALISE better when she's in the throes of astral copulation with trans-dimensional entities or arranging fuck aktions with false libertines that culminate in their brutal murder at the hands of a deranged ex-wrestler in color-inverted clown make-up.*

guillotine catapult. pandemic stage envy. impulse construct brining the gruel lattice. god speed whip-crackers pull rank degrees in firm accordance with procedural asphyxiation like a battering ram through a packing peanut. DNA pressurized chapped esophagus. raw glitching ether of caustic phosphorus. bowel widow embalmed in clothesline; curled folds hardening when pussies needs a cleanse.

*while researching the probable cause for the inward barrage that has begun to hasten his physical degradation, KIRITSIS stumbled upon a name that was new, even to an arcane information sponge like himself; CYSYTISISM.*

*according to leaked documents from the New Normal, under the surface of the multiverse there was the GOREGAZE; a network of cosmic bleeds that enveloped the fabric of the universe after the expansion of PARAREICH; the resulting entity that came when GARMONGHAZI, LYCANIVVE, and JANRUMACH fused in a swirl and grew to copulate with HAZARAG NOMUNAC; the membrane-caped crab-legged floating torso that broke the seal at the end of existence, suspended in the white void like a superhero emblem. this completed the SHOCK LOAD; an event that served to join the realities of the multiverse in a single shared experience that didn't vary in the slightest.*

*who and what didn't survived the SHOCK LOAD became absorbed into a floating stain of caustic detritus described by the New Normal as a "Reflux Plume". the New Normal called this plume CYSYTISISM, named after an alleged secret society frequently referenced in deeper dives of New Normal documents. details of the society are scarce, but it was once rumored to have members of both the Spamin and Titanal families in their most elite tier.*

*(side note; some claim that 1930s pulp magazine creator Silvio Rotpule had intimate knowledge of the Cysytisism Society, even incorporating their crest; a bladed star or rose with a dripping rat skull in its center, into the symbol sewn to the robes of the SKULL VERMIN KLAN, a guild of animal-masked villains from the thirteenth GLOOM novel, and was intending to weave the information into the mythos of that series, suggesting that the title character was*

*born of a sex rite involving a young couple and paradimensional entities. Rotpule disappeared before this entry in the series could be finished. a handwritten outline occasionally makes the rounds among the more monkish annotators of superhero lore, but its authenticity cannot be proven. it should also worth referencing that Rotpule's novels were published by Anulling Titan Syndicate, which was owned and operated by media magnate Jorges Titanal... rumored to have been sexually involved with Iris Thacher, the wife of famed Dr. Elias Thacher, who passed under mysterious cardiovascular circumstances... as well as Iris' unstable sister Lucretia Nudesco, who herself would go on to marry mercurial real estate mogul Jonas Spamin, giving birth to twins Dario and Dax, the former a stillbirth that is rumored to remain conjoined somewhere on Dax's person.)*

*in the wake of the SHOCK LOAD, the research division of the New Normal, spearheaded by RINA GRISUM; their highest ranking Invalidist, managed to obtain a CYSYSTISM spore; a vascular knot of green-black protein deposit that contained trace elements of innumerable life forms, from RWOACHER ephemera scouts to a SPARAGAPCROS lice mother, all ground to a molecular debris that served to create a universal pollutant teeming with perpetually mutating strains of undiscovered parasites that could transform the physiology and psychology of their hosts with glacially casual hostility.*

*the next piece of information seemed only tangentially related to KIRITSIS' research, but nonetheless it piqued the interest of that part of us that most keep concealed beneath a gauze of regularity, but has willfully overridden much of KIRITSIS' bottomless need for prurient discovery. a clip that was posted on Deep Web Macumba named* "INCELIPHATE OBTAINS VIDEO OF SALOME THRILWELL PERFORMING CYSYSTISM RITUAL" *from a user named BLACKPILLAR13;*

*two blandly pretty women dressed like senators gradually mutilate a hanged prepubescent girl with gleaming steak knives. they fillet the girl's face and then take turns wearing it like a mask. a text-crawl at the bottom of the screen suggests this is designed to deliver a shock load of deliberate terror with the intention of causing the child's body to release an oxidation product into her bloodstream which will serve as the secret ingredient for the elixir needed to complete the ritual of CYSYTSISM.*

*the handsome duo of madame senators (neither of which resemble Thrilwell, for the record), now red-faced from the child-skin-facial trade, squeeze the girl's veins until their contents are rung out into the inflatable kiddie pool beneath her feet. they then scoop the nightmare-carbonated gore-flow into ornate pimp goblets that have been bejeweled with human baby teeth, toasting the climax as the ritual insists.*

*KIRITSIS didn't see any mention of such a "ritual" in the New Normal documents, and on closer inspection the clip looks plagiarized from a key scene in the film* FOUR LIVE BEES FEEDING ON TEARS INSIDE A WOMAN'S EYE, *a Danish/Italian co-production from Stanley Vertreffn and Vincenzo Scappeli. the names "Inceliphate" and "BLACKPILLAR13" also clue him into the exceedingly likely possibility that this yet another mediocre prank from the wearyingly contrarian Alt-Right troll brigades. nothing to learn here.*

cut fluffer. terminally moralistic puritan scum gristle are narcissistically fixated on their willful degradation. disinfectant shades compress the toy's warp; gunning clag from all their lowered blood. springboard rake fire. titanium disappointment threshold. sunken mud-church of kerosene cherubs. amoebic breaches hooded their snouts on pinpricks of foaming bell; an industrial sludge nightmare symphony course-correcting the battery-dewed vapors wafting from their landmine-voided cum-spores until their diarrhetic glitching settles into the shape of a moaning fetus armored in scabrous golden rinds.

*with a lid strapped tight on his persistent unnamed yearings, KIRITSIS spent the late evening / early morning furthering the already overlong editing process of his generationally gestating* WET RENALDA *barrage tape compilation... consisting primarily of the more unusual segments from* RENALDA TALAG; *a late-morning talk show that aired during the peak of the 1990s "Trash TV" craze, spliced between his favorite scenes from* WET MARKETS; *a multi-volume series of mondo videos from the Japanese underground.*

*the* WET MARKETS *series was compiled and distributed by NYUNOMARU , who would eventually move on to producing and releasing extreme Ero Guro OVA titles, starting with the utterly hate filled* EVIL HERO SHAW: BODY HOLE PLUCKER. WET MARKETS *however, promised only reality... lingering on the blood and panic stirred "up from mankind's underside in the reproductive wake of its willowing flesh crimes".*

*KIRITSIS purchased the found art murder porn from a sketchy kiosk at the Star Rose Mall over a two year period, just before the labyrinthian retail compound began its slow slide into time lapse footage of post-gothic ruin; a walk-through marble husk of eroding consumer confidence in Brobdingnagian corporeal form. the kiosk was manned by a petite young lady who always wore backless shirts as to show off her ornate back tattoo; a barcode-faced figure peaking from an emerald cloak of foaming waves.*

{VOID}

*the first volume in the series KIRITSIS was able to obtain was actually its 13th, titled "SHOCK LOOKERS OF THE RAPE LOAD". the tape culminated with a live birth. a pregnant woman had gone into labor and was delivering the baby in the back of a car parked on the side of the road. as the baby is crowning her dilated vagina, a large truck skids and loses control, crashing into the car. baby's neck gets snapped, their head now dangling like a wet red lantern. the woman is screaming and whining before bursting with a sudden surge of eagerness to void her torn orifice of the stunted broken corpse.*

*when KIRITSIS was in grade school, he became quite adept at over-enunciating a mild headache until he was able to even convince himself that he was firmly in the throes of a severe head cold. the house would then be all his, and he would tape what was then the most readily available access line to gorge his burgeoning prurience; the* RENALDA TALAG *show. the host was Renalda Talag; a somewhat well-known B-Movie actress best known for playing the lead role of "Angie Thacher" in* LUNAR RASH *and a bit later as "Melora Soavi"; the final girl of* SOW.

*Talag would find much greater infamy on the syndicated "trash TV" circuit of the late 90s, where she would interview a series of guests that ranged from the freakish to the criminal. regular topics of conversation included well-worn tabloid exposes of the day; aliens, child abductions, interviews with porn stars and shock rockers (the "lost episode" of Flint Rupture's meltdown when confronted by a member of the audience who accused him of stealing his whole act was a favorite of KIRITSIS), suburban cults and hidden societies (much of the time devoted to Gift Givers, since disbanded), urban folklore and/or fakelore depending on one's own tower of belief (the episode on SECTAPHARM sightings ended up looping back to the cult discussion, this time pertaining to the Communilogians, also disbanded).*

*Talag's most talked about string of episodes devoted an entire week to the terroristic arch-criminal THE GUIGNOL, interviewing survivors, historians, and even former associates (who appeared under a blue-dot veil of voice modulated anonymity). this string of shows only aired once, as during the finale the network signal was hacked, and the episode was interrupted by a strobing flash of gruesome footage from slaughterhouses, extreme BDSM pornography, and reams of bizarre text, all overlayed with bowel-churning feedback and atonal groaning. KIRITSIS was fortunate enough to be home that week, and the dubbed tape remains a crown jewel amidst the sum total of his homebody ephemera.*

*after this, RENALDA TALAG steered its program away from the dark and the bizarre and chose to focus on the mercurial hostilities of subliterate trailer park residents, casually vindictive celebrity gossip, and "i was a geek but now i'm chic!" makeover tutorials.*

*KIRITSIS' initial plan was to submit the* WET
RENALDA *barrage tape to the local network
Channel 11 for their late night block of paid
programming, but since the start of tape's gestation,
ownership of the network has changed hands a few
times, and after the events of 9/11, local networks
shied away from any programming deemed
controversial, strange, violent, challenging, or
trading in prurient sexual expression. the cathode
iniquity that was after hours basic cable just doesn't
exist anymore... replaced instead with algorithmic
mudflows of redundant sitcoms, played blockbusters,
bland tabloids, and smarmy "adult" cartoons.*

renal stag. decapitated wasp flies holding its severed
head. zip-tied to a guardrail. cunt run down with
bowling balls. crawlspace seed maturating
overgrowth. carrion tubing in the rain-thinned silver
mung. bubbling spittle course magnesia-rake the
sewer moons.

*right about now, KIRITSIS could go for being held in
place on the floor by the palm of his hands with the
heels of a pair of stiletto boots glacially digging past
the skin, coring the muscle, and scraping the bone on
their way to the floor... screams being muffled with a
zipper-teethed leather mound.*

in slack. schadenfreude exile. mermaid taxidermy.
serotonin pangs from giddy revenge. asphalt habit.

gonzo credentials. char marbled in the dropper thumb-knuckles plunged into the eye. beige gorilla drag. above-the-fray posturing is a clear indication of mediocrity in extremis. no opinion zone. the formlessly petulant hostility of superhero-adjacent catastrophe porn. release the cassowaries.

*of all the viscous wraiths occupying the malignant seedbeds of KIRITSIS' corrosive inner terrain, unendingly wet with the voracious dread of matter-of-fact ugliness, none pronounce themselves with more magnificent lunging perversity than MAITRESSE DELIA; the varicose marbled mayoral crone-saint of GROMORRAH.*

*the truth of MAITRESSE DELIA's past remains tightly gauzed within her. substituting for confirmed knowledge, word-of-mouth myth making will have to satisfy the ceaseless gorging of the information void.*

*having never shaved due to a severe case of psoriasis, MAITRESSE DELIA's arms and legs are thick with black hairs, flaky from the molting pink flesh they were grown to conceal. her face is hard and sour, a cluster of raspberry bulbed goiters hanging off the kitchen-knife edge of her left cheek. she keeps her salt-and-pepper hair short, the scalp sporadically pocked with bumps that resemble half-coiled potato bugs, the psoriatic formations most concentrated a few inches above her right ear, where a part might be had her hair been fuller. her mouth has been fitted with dentures that were laminated in gummed pennies she had melted down and poured across them, hardening into muddy copper that resembled a battery corroded by its own acid.*

*MAITRESSE DELIA is rumored to have been the catalyst of a minor "zombie outbreak" that occurred in Hawntag a couple of years back; an occurrence which proved to be easily contained and draggingly uneventful, inspiring little more than meandering town halls and grimy horror metal mixtapes. the origin of how and why she could have done this remains as unclear as the arch of any cinematic retread of living dead pathos, so perhaps it's best not to revisit such groan-filled coma inducer episodes of the area's history.*

*known for its meager beach head of crusted rheum and dead skin cells, where the dead worlds of the multiverse are a single visible moon, the architecturally inclined Baba Yaga restructured the garbage island of GROMORRAH into something of a gated community for many varieties of malodorous morlocks who would rather not frustrate themselves with hopeless bids for attaining fraternity among the more well-established subterranean contingents of the area; who despite their "you do you" platitudes, still insist on the reinforcement of the stifling base decorum's and nigh-unachievable aesthetic expectations of the "normie" societal clubhouses that act as the generalized surface targets for their entry-*

*level hacktivist lash.*

*how KIRITSIS himself enters the picture (and how MAITRESSE DELIA enters him) stretches back yet again to an episode of* RENALDA TALAG, *which focused on the controversy surrounding the area's "Floating Stain" of Gromorrah.*

*for the program's climatic stinger, Talag and her crew actually visited the piecemeal barge, adventuring across and going deep within the rotting plastic jungle. numerous translucent bags were shredded on branches of jagged metal. when they blow in the wind they resemble the ghosts of children who became impaled on the shards after failing to reach the top of the trash mountain. used diapers were arranged atop stalks of aluminum like puffed flowers presenting their clumpy brown pollen.*

*just before the end of the footage, one of Talag's camera men catches a glimpse of a figure. the figure appears in shape and movement to be a mature woman, wrapped in plastic from head to toe, wearing a mask fashioned from the pages of a supermarket tabloid, conveniently scouring a few feet behind Talag herself. Talag attempts contact to get an interview, but the figure scurries away at a speed normally reserved for encounters with deadly prey.*

*"was that the 'Maitresse Delia' our viewers and guests told us about?"*

Online Bible Class Bombarded with Sick Porn. amoebas serrate diagnostic plaster, sharpening the erosion of illuminating faculties. with the abeyance of a heavy bag, their cunt starts breeding flies. canned pasta aged twenty five years bulbed the comb with liquid wool. inner thighs slick with dew from violent night rips hasten a thaw mutations annulled. mounting scrapes. scarab crosshairs. key-length of gooseflesh walks the styrene rifle scope.

*KIRITSIS can only recall his inaugural trespass beyond the pale in fast-forward tumble of jagged snow unfolding in a flashing ream;*

*toast colored wallpaper... papery night gown.... a woman who strongly resembled Lene Cruaton; the concubin-ic hard-right ragdoll whose physical appearance could only be described as a deflated carwash tube man draped in half between the maw of a wire hanger.... cocking head volleying between hasty reactions of splenetic defensiveness and cascading bewilderment... a sharp face breaking against the corner of a coffee table... recently shampooed hair being long enough to wrap around the throat two times over... the amplified huskiness of their groans after the first sharp punch just beneath the sternum... pressing feet down between the shoulders blades, bending back their arms, moving the feet to the back of the head, and hammering their face into checkered linoleum... tea kettle on stovetop... whistling... shrieking.... dragging smashed cunt by the frazzled dripping scalp... studying the boiling water... how the clear pot and the blue flame made it look like stained glass being melted down into a bubbled puddle... how it hissed like angry vipers when it vacated the kettle.... bile-lunged shouts... ramped-up time lapse of forming blisters.... poking the blisters with a sewing needle... draining the blisters into dixie cups.... feeding their content into a syringe... feeding its content to their eyeball...*

*KIRITSIS clad himself in what would become integral to future "aktualizations" of his overwhelming need to transgress;*

*- a pair of shiny leather sneakers.*

*- a pair of grey workpants that have been made into cut-offs*

*- a pair of dark brown leather driving gloves*

*- a rotation of XL band and movie poster t-shirts with the collars and sleeves snipped off.*

*- a white anonymous sex-party mask with 3 strips of duct tape over the mouth (one in a straight line, two forming an X over the line) and a symbol drawn thriteen times over the face; a V with three sharp lines forming an S on its left and two sharp lines forming a K on its right, which when studied uveil a fusion of all the letters in KIRITSIS' name, merged into an emblematic ink-carved rune.*

{VOID}

*- all worn over a form-hugging nylon body stocking that shifts in the light between gradients of metallic blue.*

*this would briefly become known as the uniform of the monster the media would go on to christen with the tabloid ready nomenclature of "THE SURREAL KILLER".*

empathy deficit. thick veins creaking blood logged shank. grips fan out to web a bowl. furloughed greetings renew episode of fondled sockets pulling rank. base snared by rim contracting in jest. bod is a gullet.

*when KIRITSIS finds himself located within a secured zone of guard-relieving comfort, the full breadth of his gruesome aptitudes first bristle the edges of his hairlip, then dilate the pores of his vulturine head to circle above him in a spatte-rusted halo of fungal balloons on kite strings of popping veins.*

"We put Corey Taylor and Randy Blythe in a room and asked them how they'd save metal"

if the answer is anything other than "fill this room with flocks of alarmed cassowaries and don't open the door until there is nothing but bleak silence", then you ain't saving *SHIT*.

flypaper shibari. convenient amnesia in an artful slow burn of rolling echoes. indefinite seclusion unearths the paved sensitivities of self-frustrating joy-killers who explosively spiral into ballistic frenzy when bottomless access to limitless cultural expansion falls ever so short in meticulously validating and/or tempering their unquenchable entitlement, terminal neediness, malignant narcissism, and shallow resentment.

*KIRITSIS knows perhaps better than anyone what a struggle it can be to find a partner who doesn't recoil in objection when opening up about your daily habit of skull-fucking briefly microwaved mannequin heads that have been boosted from the display case of a Baby Gap.*

Charlotte Gainsbourg wears a strap-on in bed with Asia Argento. needles scrape in the key of Symphony No.7 in A major op.92. the juice of a plump cherry stains a heart across the lip. enjoy this vortex of unfulfilled potential, ya tramp.

*as this pleadingly mandated interaction hiatus continues its shanking elongation of indeterminate climax... the meaty breath of its morning yawn increasingly stale with the slow-weeping rot of snapped-off teeth neglected of repair... KIRITSIS can't help but to become over-surged with vengeance-brained schadenfreude... to have any lingering pangs of empathy violently silenced by the bleachered impulse of a my-time-now snarl... to wedge himself deep into the crawlspace frontier of the collective societal sulk... grunting caustic reams of harsh phobics while lung-buttered fists grind into blur just below the gut's paunch.... orgasm rendered neon pink from traces of blood.... unsettled rawness sinking bone... delighted with the scaly hangnail tatters... the fold-trapped spits drying into a mossy fuzz... a fungal stalk telepathically groan-shrieking as infants do when having been retrieved from the sludge-wet maw of a hyper-localized grease fire.... reparations for a childhood spent locked in frustrated quietude.... the healthiest form of retreat from those verbalized bulldozers that were always manned by the complainers and victimizers who never fucking lose yet still cast themselves as working class freedom-fighting "an attack on me is an attack on all" revolutionaries when the most remotely meager of challengers approaches... KIRITSIS knows they will never breach the satisfied contentment he achieves from indulging his readily available tastes.*

post-traumatic cringe dispassionately mauled with halting caution. those on the bleeding edge of unrestrained sadism gaze upon his works in repulsed awe; reclaiming the lore mutations purloined.

penal ills. piled tensions disqualified from a grant of release out of concern of inadvertent insult. the wounded mumbling of bodied labors core a tubercular scraper of ganglia wave pools down the suckling gorge of their stigmatic gullet with smarm-doctored vocal cadences licked so heavy in bile and venom that the listener feels as if the sides of their head have been smeared to the point of encasement with the mucosal residue of completion-seizing reptilian nectar.

conflict tourist. almost had me convinced enough to imbue the guts' reflex with something other than piteous loathing to the scribed climax of your willed abeyance. percolating rheum.  excrement forked where the hollow dipped to berate with silence the chalking of a slug.

hype man for an eyeball in a jar. juiced leather webs the band-aid. continuity czars ground to their skulls by the molten iron tread of mythos' spear-toothed roiling. veal hindquarters cut-spiced with baby cage meal. heads are fleshed in mold and clown-painted with grime from between the tiles of a public bathroom. cockroach abdomens have the same consistency as peanut butter wafer cookies.

panic laureate. hook-looped twine choking sprout of syruped pig. wandering porn bleeds out the painted screen. stagnation irrigates abandoned traumas weeding through the rupture's mask. a dead shell animated only by parasites.

cellulite clefts. petri dish carrion ranks poached to furnish and swell. the middle of her name is "lie", as in "lie still while you're piped with fishhooks". baby skull Hitachi wand mummified in thigh gaps positioned to burst from the cunt's mouth upon completion's shriek. i would not hit a woman. i would hit all the women. love me how I want you to love me or I'll kill you.

... wrestling on a kitchen floor... shirtless... black leggings... fabric latticed with rips.... scalp fluffed in clawing hands... pulled head arches neck.... lobbing mask from lung... hole in face piston-fucked... fingers cupping ass... material snagged in hangnails... slipped in drool on the tiles... constrictive throat-back... forehead butting lower stomach... chin brushing sack-grit... plasmic enamel comb... part in the hair mohawked by cordyceps of ejaculate... macing eyeballs until socket erupt carbonated pink milk... tear-streak burn scars indenting baby fat cheek flesh... gloved thumbs hook inside fizzing ocular wounds... temples in palm-vice... tighten grip on pouring head... jaw and cock as the merge-point of the priapic splicer...

*despite the easy availability of hi-definition modern pornography accessible to any device, KIRITSIS still finds the greatest assistance to relieving his onanistic impulses in revisiting* STEAMED CANDY: *a film released during the tail end of the narrative pornographic feature's "Golden Age".*

*written and directed by Selena Murifalt (made in between the animated* SNUFF THE COCK MEETS WATERFOUL *and the 'mainstream' horror film* LUNAR RASH), STEAMED CANDY *stars the eternally ravishing Deliah Valise as Candice; the sole female employee at the Blue Charm Candy Factory. Candice has a long simmering crush on her shift manager Florence, played by Lydon Atello (Deliah's real-life partner, known on the grey market tape trading circuit for his COPRAPIXIE series of rape-fetish shit play films). attempts to flirt are clumsy on Candice's end, as she is easily overwhelmed by her suppressed desires to engage in extreme acts of kink with Florence. these fantasies play out within the private universe of Candice, which are staged for the viewer to digest.*

*after several amorous vignettes that take place entirely inside Candice's mind, she eventually works herself up into such a frenzy that she finally corners Florence in his office, laying herself bare in the figurative and literal. Florence is of course flushed with erotic excitement, and the two are off to the races, with Candice squirming-ly eager to act out the scenarios that have shock-loaded her neural floodgates. things however take a drastic turn, as it turns out Florence isn't too interested in following Candice's meticulous detail, turning disagreeable and belligerent. the tryst grows more menacing, with Florence not pulling his punches on Candice, spanking and whipping and jamming his cock up and down her "greedy fuck tubes" (to quote Florence).*

*the scene culminates with Florence dragging Candice by her hair across the floor and down a flight of steps, stopping at a vat of melted sucking candies. Florence cuffs Candice's ankles and wrists, placing her on a conveyer belt. Florence dips a ladle into the vat of bubbling liquid sugar. he returns to Candice and pours the boiling substance up and down her body. at first she screams, but soon she is breathing with grit-teethed anger, which eventually morphs into hate-fucked guttural arousal. after several minutes of this torture, Deliah Valise finally unlocks that trademark vicious dominatrix side she had concealed throughout her performance as Candice, snarling acerbic projectiles of linguistic laceration at Lydon Atello's Florence:*

*"That all you got, baby dick? you gimpy faggot? you fucking CANDY ASS!?!"*

*well now it's a fucking challenge. Florence gets up on top of Candice, but not before uncuffing her ankles so he can get up inside of her. Candice wraps her legs around Florence's waist, squeezing tightly, bucking up into him. he struggles to breath as Cadnice continues hurling vindictive insults and cat calls at him.*

*"that hurt, fuck-face? stupid cunt can't breathe, huh? c'mon big shot; fucking rape my ass! harder you fuck! frost my shit you worthless pussy.... i'm not choking yet! i'm not fucking choking yet!"*

*Florence begins to shudder and convulse, but is unable to pull out of Candice, as she is still gripping him tight. when he is finished cumming, Candice throws him to the ground with her legs. as he lays on the floor, Candice shits Florence's cum out of her ass and on to his perma-grinning face. she then drags his blissfully comatose body over to the vat of boiling melted candy. Candice picks up Florence and dumps his body in the vat, which snaps him out of his daze, causing him to thrash around in the burning liquid sugar before he sinks to the bottom, crippled from searing pain.*

*the movie ends with Candice starting up the machines in the factory, the contents of the vat being squirted onto the conveyer belt to later harden into pieces of ribboned candy. the final shot is Candice unwrapping a piece of candy to seductively place on her tongue with a sinister wink of the eye.*

*a recently released Blu-Ray / DVD combo pack from the boutique cult film distributer DEGRANULATE (which would come to replace KIRITSIS' own worn out VHS dub from when the film aired on the Blue Rose Network) features a wide-ranging commentary track provided by Selena Rotuple (formerly Murifalt) and arthouse terror Stanley Vertreffen, who cites* STEAMED CANDY *as one of his sources of inspiration for* CHROME COVERS; *his highly controversial deconstructionist take on the erotic film genre. the film is also cited by adult filmmaker Aevea Within as had having a tremendous impact on her after having been introduced to her by Vincenzo*

*Scappeli during the conceptual process of* WITHIN A STAR IS TORN. *Within has expressed interest in doing an updated version of* STEAMED CANDY, *but so far the project remains in a stasis of development.*

curbside pregnancy vaccine. anxiety spikes in the beading months. pine combs like turds of lizard skin. heavily considering licking the blood of your children off the business-end of a night stick. an arm without a hand graft below the navel. i hope a Black Bloc loots your colon with hedge-clippers, you ear-wax textured dildoloid. it's not getting worse; it's getting filmed.

*KIRITSIS spent the bulk of his teen years at THE FRACTURE COMPOUND; a militarized nickname for the Chalk Heart of Gromorrah.*

*before Gromorrah drifted out to sea, it was connected to the island, situated like a raspberry bulbed growth dangling from the seam that divided the counties of Suasan and Fulsok. when the Hawntag Youth Outreach Center closed in disgrace after unwillingly booking the pedo-core band Victim Impact Statement, the Compound became the spot for the area's more right-brain inclined teens to congregate. a number of artists, musicians, actors, poets, and filmmakers would emerge from the compound, as would several high profile criminals, killers, cultists, domestic terrorists, and mental patients, most of whom ended up incarcerated at Thacher Memorial, which has been shuttered and cordoned off after a violent uprising sometime in the late 2000s.*

*KIRITSIS documented his time at the compound in a series of marble notebooks, each entry increasing in their erratic frenzy. he used these musings as grist for the mills of his lyrical / vocal contributions to ANTHROPAPHARRIDAN; the free form art / music / video project that was localized entirely within Gromorrah. KIRITSIS' piece, titled "Homicide Shrines", was the group's most unhinged and aggressive composition, and to this day it's the only performance of the ANTHROPAPHARRIDAN collective that has been documented on video and cassette.*

*("Homicide Shrines" was later cited as source of inspiration for Richey Walker and Chiaki Fujiwara's "Sewer Moons" collaboration, as both artists were frequent weekend visitors to the Fracture Compound).*

*as for Gromorrah's most famous resident, MAITRESSE DELIA didn't seem to object or even acknowledge the presence of these costume gypsies and self-tortured theater kids, opting to remain in her living quarters at the end of the Fracture Compound's longest hallway. she did however take notice of several patrons who she would sense as being genuinely unique, and took them under her wing, eventually revealing the lived-in secrets of the island. this handpicked class would be come to be referred to as "The Special Interests" by the more catty and jealous inhabitants of Gromorrah, whose presence was ascertained to have more to do with achieving (and later exploiting) the kind of inverted status that inevitably putrefies all creative communities.*

*of that curated class, two students stood out to MAITRESSE DELIA as encapsulating the opposing extremes of her own private universe. for her monkish devotion to all the teachings down to the micro-crevices between the spaces of the letters of the words, class valedictorian VALISE ROTPULE represented the determined obsession to streamline reality into a single seamless cult object. for his ill-begotten calling to obtain obscure knowledge frequently becoming overwhelmed by shakingly frustrated episodes of cosmically scattershot aloofness. CARLTON KIRITSIS represented the restlessly unfocused impulse to consume and absorb disparate ephemera, becoming a crossroad for the colliding detritus of the universe.*

*on KIRITISIS' last night at Gromorrah, which also his 19th birthday, was spent in what was known as THE CRAWLSPACE FRONTIER; a series of tunnels within the walls of the compound. at first appearing to be lined with innumerable small mirrors, upon closer inspection they were revealed to be micro-screens peering into what seemed to be alternate realities.*

*KIRITSIS absorbed as much imagery as he could, and channeled what he saw onto the page. this became the manuscript* RED VELVET YEAST, *which he struggled to get published in a fashion that would meet his meticulous specificities. the closest he came to achieving validation was through VILLATION PRESS, a relationship that ended before it began when KIRTISIS' innate volatility came up against the performative hostility of transgressive publisher JAMESON WILPRAF.*

*the manuscript was eventually bootlegged, "stolen by an intern" as Wilpraf told KIRITSIS in secret. and passed around the area, credited to "AUTHOR UNKNOWN". that "intern' would come to be revealed as D.W. CAMMBUA, who would launch his own publishing house CONJUGAL APPARITION PRESS on the strength of the first "official" release of* RED VELVET YEAST, *which just so coincidently happened to arrive at the same time as a disastrous "alt-horror-porn" film adaptation of the book was announced by Wilpraf's newest venture; a boutique cult film distributor called VILIFIED BLUE. now simply titled* RED YEAST; *a title that even KIRITSIS admits wishes he would've named the original manuscript, the film was only notable for an early appearance by adult film megastar AEVEA WITHIN. to this day, KIRITSIS has refused to view the film.*

finished choking down the film *SOILED DOVES AND THE TOTES MCGOATS AMAZEBALLS RECALIBRATION OF BUNNY BOILER:* an unfunny, unsexy, unimaginative adapatation of the Cool Ranch Comics all-female superhero team, directed with some vague eye for visual dramatics by newcomer Anna Kimikis (her previous feature *Swinegrave* still hasn't secured a release outside of the Indonesian arthouse festival circuit), but unfortunately micro-managed to frustrating mediocrity by the powers-that-be at Castletop Pictures, desperate to cash-in on whatever woke-scolds are still out there demanding that every single fictional cartoon lady be "liberated from the male gaze" (ah yes... the photosensitive holo-caustal evil that is "the male gaze", where women are adored and worshipped for achieving the bare-minimum of existence by introverted voyeurs who have been forced to compartmentalize their lusts in order to avoid spending the remainder of their days in stressed-out terrified exile as punishment for the crime of having eyes and a cock).

The Soiled Doves themselves (Eye Candy, Predatriesse, Detective Rosaline Lagat) end up bit players in their own story, as their presence becoming overwhelmed by the Horror Show / Red Pillar villainess Bunny Boiler; a one-time ancillary character in the CRC Universe (the "bottom bitch" of voodoo clown pimp Papa Spank) who took on a life of her own, becoming a rabid fan favorite and flagship character of the company, but whose solo adventures frequently become tiresome to the point of aggrieved physical exhaustion.

in their comic book iterations, the characters each have distinctive outfits, abilities, personality traits, and layered backstories. because the studio doesn't respect either the source material or whatever audience their might be for this material, every character ends up wearing thrift store ensembles, with only the most miniscule hint of their graphic novel counterparts allowed in their look, all while possessing the same glib sarcastic butthole personality as every other cinematic superhero (male or female). even a cracked out performance by Ben Thomas Geysourke as the film's villain Sarin Athanor feels labored. an aggravating chore all around.

in need of a palette-cleanser, i was able to catch the inaugural episode of *SAVAGE BRUTALITY WRESTLING*, a new promotion that emerged in the wake of Legalized Violence Wrestling shuddering its doors after years of financial struggle and behind-the-scenes power plays, its demise hastened after Rita Talag (aka "Talia Splatter") murdered Justin Boumrash (aka "Rashomon Justice") and their two young children before drowning herself (the ever presence of this particular factoid makes the SBW's use of "Pazi Sta Radis" by Wiklah Sky as their theme music particularly insensitive, though those who pick up on the reference more than likely won't clue the uninitiated into exactly why this is so). the personnel behind SBW are mostly transplates from LVW, and the program does indeed carry over much of the feel and performers of that company, albeit propped up by the billionaire tech-giant Chance Cave; owner of Serengheti.com.

about halfway through the program, after a violent hoss-fest between Mordred Wakes and Mutomaki the Lifer (on loan from the TOKYO FIST promotion in Japan), a vignette plays. the images play like a dead world travelogue; scrap metal, abandoned cars, animal skeletons and lizard skins... all arranged like an outsider art installation curated by irradiated bag ladies.

"a deep shade of blue / is always there"

suddenly the soundtrack swells over the jagged detritus: "the Sun Ain't Gonna Shine )(Anymore)" by the Walker Brothers. a group of men and women, originally positioned as scarecrows wearing white masks with black tape over the mouth, dressed in the tattered regalia of wasteland scavengers, come down from their perches and creep-walk toward a tower of piled-up motor homes. the scarecrow revolt reaches the front of the tower and stops, removing their white masks, wearing grins that alternate between vengeful sneer and amorous thirst. on their foreheads there is a crude emblem; the letter F with the letter S drawn beneath the two lines of the F.

on the front porch, a large bald man sits in a desk

chair. he stands up before his congregation. he is wearing grey dress pants, brown fingerless gloves, reddish leather shoes, and no shirt; a crabbed scrawl of sentence fragments and unusual symbols tattooed all over his bare skin; most concentrated around the width of his arms. he raises his head, its flesh chalked with psoriasis, no doubt made more extreme with make-up and prosthetics. his meat dead gaze locks on the camera in front of him, eyes swirling with blood and gore from the images being projected over him.

the screen crashes to black, soundtrack shifting to "Prayer to God" by Shellac, with big red letters that resemble cutter marks on teenage wrists being slashed across the screen;

*SOON.*

*FRANCO SECT.*

*ENJOY.*

*c. SBW/Serengheti.com*

LONG ISLAND VIDEO 13 NEWS REPORTING: the law office of Grolman and Postap on Bannon Ave in Windlab, NY became the latest entry in the gruesome encyclopedia of American rage attacks, as 9 clerks and 3 lawyers were violently slashed in their cubicles and offices by an assailant wielding a pair of large machetes.

a fourth lawyer, Mackenzie Lohmoc, was killed in her office, the whole ordeal captured on her computer camera, as she was in a teleconference. a knife was stabbed through her hand, connecting her to the desk. her arm was then broken in half at the elbow. then she was strangled with the cord of her mouse, and finally the assailant drove a large knife or small sword through the top of her head. her attacker then looked into the security camera and waved their hand in front of their masked face. the footage then skips ahead thirteen seconds, and the perp is no longer in the office.

connected to the attack is the recent murder of Ann Dara-Proushaythe, a manager at that same law office, who was a victim of a severe home invasion. the thorough brutality of these murders has detectives looking into the employment history of the office for any disgruntled ex-workers.

a suspect has yet to be named, as the perp concealed his or her identity behind a mask. the mask itself fits the description reported by eye witnesses to the crime scene of the Proushaythe slaying; something similar to those seen in the films "Eyes Wide Shut" and "Chrome Covers", only with strips of tape X'd across the mouth and marked up with scratches.

the namesakes of the firm; Stuart Grolman and Celina Postap, could not be reached for comment.

more as this story develops.

This week in summation; finally get to make a legit roast beef sammich. plopped it down on a plate full of cat food.

"if you were tasked with making us toast, there'd be bones in it."

gout lines. wood of the desk pasted to palm-skin by driven kitchenware plotting its vomit. vermin-cord sinks in the chin-lard; liquid hatchets sweating mud to part their cartilage.

recirculating ancient prejudices. everyone with Alzheimer's is just fucking with you. the greatest trick the right ever pulled was convincing themselves that using their tongues to laminate the anal cavities of those who own the universe is an act of taboo-breaking subversion.

Blast Beat David Spades. jaundice eyes crushed to sparks reprise in the glimmer of stress-eaten reflux. the rubber skin and condom lips are gone from age. sexual offending as a way of undermining social norms. sanity, relaxation, and enjoyment are all punishable by community-sanctioned rape.

infection dynamics. i cannot recall a time before wanting to kill. if i had a nickel for every time someone told me "i understand how frustrated you are", i'd have enough to buy the appropriate number of ax-handles to accurately demonstrate. black hairclips pinching rib-flesh like swarms of fluttering insects. limb-braided spokes jump on their spins, inviting perverted blood to a bizarre orgy. a lot of people are very fortunate that i have a hatred of guns.

*Q: what do you get when you hire someone for a part time position, dangle the carrot of a full time position in front of them, then after ten years decide instead to cut their hours in half?*

*A: I'm not sure what you get, but I hope it's malignant and inoperable.*

... parting dimensional slip... inverted ballistics balkanized containment.... a plastic spray bottle of industrial grade disinfectant has been ornamented with no less than thirteen syringes... their plungers like the segmented eyes of a stalking cartoon... ...breaking beyond.... beading trickle stains cheekbone... ...marinates in the haze of an exiting out-call... appropriating peril of night terrors... a fade of fuck-you money, free television, shallow outrage, and serotonin as a guided weaponry network.... it grows alarmingly imperative that i remain averse to skirting the margins of categorical rage-murder cliches.... that light at the end of the tunnel is a Saharan dust plume of malformed forgotten brains recovered from the basement of an abandoned state-run mental hospital that has since been converted into a shopping mall...

*"Lisperal Demoncrack Anarcholes want America to be devoured by CommieFa Socialism!"* - headline from the *Sassy Cad Blortetin*

yeah sure, and i want to titty-fuck Alexandra Daddario until my dick sheds like a serpent... don't mean it gonna happen.

METAL SCENE APPARENTLY STILL POPULATED BY A WEARYING ABUNDANCE OF FAILED SATIRISTS WHOSE MISGUIDED THIRST FOR EDGY RENEGADE GODHOOD AS LED THEM TO INADVERTENTLY SUPPORT A BELIEF SYSTEM THAT WISHES TO SEE THEM GROUND INTO A PATE TO BE FED TO WHITE JESUS AND GOD MAMMON : FILM AT 11

{VOID}

...depression's depression... occupying a static husk... i've seen the face that has peered down at a Boko Haram Ransom Demand's worth of aspiring beauty pageant contestants... choke-etched in grey matter crackle... emerging in the biopsied-wake of a child molesting fast food mascot bricking into a vat of radioactive chum... dead woman chained to the walls masked in a wax skeleton on the other side of my waking rot... deep inside hard exposure to its weeping eyesore bloom... cruising this platform and finding nothing but indecisive waifs and priapic meatheads does little to temper this roiling misanthropy that sporadically threatens to subsume the totality of my temperamental intensities... i can't help but speculate if indulging this compartment of my identity has amounted to little more than an invariably frustrating waste of time, energy, and resources... that i've been licking the wrong boots... that the "freaks" have let me down a lot harder than the "normies" ever could...

*when word and image of the massacre at the Grolman and Postap offices were inevitably grinded up by the shock-comedy chum-huggers in the bowels of the internet, many commentators... their worldview no doubt malformed from lifetimes of excessive brand consumption.. began to refer to KIRITSIS as "Shy Guy"; an reference to an ancillary character from the Super Mario Bros video game franchise, due to KIRITSIS' mask bearing an inadvertent resemblance to the stout, hooded adversaries.*

*when the unexpurgated footage of the assault found its way onto the algorithms of DEEP WEB MACUMBA users, it had been titled by the uploader (username PaulasPoundPiece) "SHY GUY LEVELS UP".*

fatigue anxiety. a credo victim's deep swamp revenge porn. moving accident black spot. lettering soft backs with roasted caulk; dead-skin-grey as the wet-street-skies. i have been here for as long as here has been. the ravines of my perdition propel in a brackish clack. when this is over... you will long for the comfort of the gutter.

*KIRITSIS once more finds himself on the other side of a stress-worn blackout. in the twitchy-and-blinky search to reclaim his faculties... ridden with trauma like ropes of cancer that bulb the legs muscles of a dying hound... he discovers that his bleary-eyed nocturnal proclivities have culminated yet again with a journey into the bowels of Long Island; quite literally.*

*steady drips of bacteria-strewn water reverberate drool-lobbed echo-crackle off the brown-green walls of the sewer tunnel... its surface blistered from chain-surges of tumbling excretea. KIRITSIS nudges the clusters of coo-squealing rodents off his grey pants, careful not to launch them into the rectal algae a few inches below them. the largest rat... easily occupying the dimensions of two full grown purse-riding chihuahuas. clings to the fabric of his navy blue M-65 field jacket. the rat's hair... dyed azure from perhaps being caught in the stream from a can of spray paint... would have enabled the creature to blend in to the coat., were it not for its tail; a lash that coiled like an overlarge potato bug, bleached into near-translucence.*

*"wanna go for a ride?"*

*as KIRITSIS locks eyes with the creature... blood-orange eyes that seem gridded like those of an insect.. the rat's disposition is that of simmering irritation. KIRITSIS puts on the jacket, the rat locked in between the shoulders. the rat then crawls to the left side of KIRITSIS, looking straight forward.*

*"you got a name?"*

*"fuckyourmouth."*

*the word(s?) the rat has spoken are laced with the detached smarm of a posturing hipster desperate to conceal their crippling existential dread with layers upon layers of deadpan party sarcasm.*

*"you kinda sound like Cocktail Frank Monyihan."*

*"isthatarealguy?"*

*"nah man he's from a movie called* DEADPAN.*"*

*"tellmeabouthim.whatishisnameiwantit."*

*"he's the shadow-side of an aspiring anti-comedian named Radley Fuches."*

*"radlyfucksisafunniernamethatcockandtailmoaningha m."*

*"so i can call you Ratley Fuches, then?"*

*"chillinlikeastraykitten."*

*KIRITSIS and RATLEY FUCHES walk down the tunnel, lost in exploration rather then consumed by escape attempts. after some time (and some frustrating back-and-forth best left to the imagination of those with a better ear for comedic trappings) they find themselves at the meeting point for several of the areas sewer lines, which resembles the ruins of a once towering metropolis that has since been paved over by a newer, colder world. brobdingnagian monuments... either mossed in shit or assembled from it... stand arranged in a line-up:*

*- a corpulent figure wearing open robes, its head that of a goat with large bat-wings for horns and a beard of octopus tentacles.*

*- a balding thin man with what looks to be a vaginal cavity grafted over his mouth.*

*- a toad-faced entity, its body a composite of faces both devastated and orgiastic.*

*- a multi-armed old woman, face consumed in a mass*

*of wiry hair, genitalia a sideways grin of chomping fangs. ("myoldfriendsandiusedtohavesexwithher", says RATLEY FUCHES. KIRITSIS too recognizes this one from a vision he had back at the Fracture Compound.)*

*- a worm ridden phallus, same size as the others, its shaft slit open to reveal innumerable orbs.*

*while KIRITSIS and RATLEY FUCHES study these monoliths, a spot of water starts to bubble between them and the statues. colored fog begins to twist off the surface of the waters, consuming the deity's in an Indonesian haze, burying them as if they were being vertically drowned in a forming dust storm. the bubbling spot eventually comes to cover the whole surface of the pipe-ushered lagoon.*

*KIRITSIS and RATLEY FUCHES adjust their sight, scanning for any spot not currently devour by steam. KIRITSIS takes notice of one large bubble in the water. it's different from the others... cloudier... more sturdy... moving upward, but not expanding, pink droplets beading on its skin. the bubble is soon revealed to be not a bubble at all, but the gleaming crown of a polished skull. the skull moves up, its black-hole eye sockets pouring out mite-heavy waters. the skull's mouth is Xed over with two pieces of chrome that mirror back a dead-world horizon. the nose of the skull is V shaped, with two lines jutting out from its left to form a K, and a crude three-lined lightning bolt forming an S or and backwards R on its right.*

*the skull walks toward KIRITSIS, now having since been abandoned by RATLEY FUCHES, who has absconded to parts unknown. with every step, the skull becomes larger, its body a liquid beanpole of discolored egg sandwich run-off, hands and feet bricked with turds. the rune on where the creature's nose would be reprises itself no less than thirteen times across its body, its imprint even left on a patch of flesh that seems to have been removed as if intended to be stitched to a quilt.*

*KIRITSIS remembers reading about such a creature before in various text on the Fracture Compound. its kind are thought to be a sort of scavenging parasite that emerged in the wake of the retribution-al sodomy CLOROPHRAGM had visited upon the NOSANGUINES and GORGRES for their myriad transgressions against the monkish ELEMPATHS. it only takes him thirteen seconds to remember their name; REVULTICKS.*

*because their mouths are seemingly bolted shut, REVULTICKS consume dead animal matter with their bodies, which are composed of gelatinous enzyme that corrodes the molecular structure of their feed, which causes them to grow in shape, weight, and size, the dimensions corresponding with the mass and volume of the matter being ingested. this one approaching KIRITSIS is beginning to look like it had feasted upon the remains of a god that had fallen into a swamp teeming with micro-organisms.*

*the REVULTICK lowers its carrion-black reservoir eyehole to KIRITSIS, inspecting him as KIRITSIS would inspect an abnormal-sized roach tangled up in the tubular fibers of an absorbent shag carpet, saturated with the accumulated sop of brushed-teeth spittle and stingy urine drips. when it becomes apparent that the REVULTICK isn't going to move, KIRITSIS steps into the ocular gulf, walking toward the red pinpoint at the end that doubles as the pupil of this mastodonic funeral home marionette... its skeleton-of-god frame yolked in the jellied vascular detritus of ruined incubation.*

*KIRITSIS scopes the texture of this cored cavern, spit-shined with oils until the walls become as a mirror. as he advances, details can begin to be spotted in the red pinpoint. long curly hair like crinkled stalks of cinnamon... cream porcelain birthmarked with cigarette burns... twin cesarean scars on either side of a paunch'd gut... suspended by a broken neck with a length of large intestine wrapped around the throat like a copperhead repurposed into a scarf... face completely masked in a bulk of flies.*

*suddenly from out of the cesarean scars, two pairs of arms burst forward, turning the dead teenager into a necrtotic human octopus. the arms reach out to the walls before them, pressing down their palms and bending their elbows, widening the gashes holding back their owners.*

*two naked women ooze from the wounds in the belly of the teenager. one is stout, face concealed behind a curtain of long greasy black hair that has been sinched around the neck, creating the impression of a fibrous cape and cowl. the other is lithe, a sweet face peeking out from a hood of horseflies, crevices dewed with some kind of candied syrup.*

*"shestartediteyouknow?"*

*RATLEY FUCHES, now roughly the size of a subway car, is directly behind KIRITSIS, who becomes so startled that his sight goes black and all he can hear is an eruptive soundtrack of crashing metal beams.*

malignacist. velvet titan. post-satirical meta-irony. cutting mesh foreskin-pink. grins at a woman in a bikini while holding a sledgehammer. how come no one talks about acid rain anymore?

*the visions in the sewer have jostled loose KIRITSIS' recollection of his favorite short-lived toy line (and accompanying requisite cartoon / mini-comic tie ins [the latter featuring some early work by Mills Moor]) from the mid-1980s; HOMUNCULORDS.*

*produced by GAUNTLEAN (the company having*

*since purchased by MAGNATE),* HOMUNCULORDS *was very much invested in adhering to the rulebook of most action figure collections targeting the boy markets of that time. the set was divided into "good guys" (the* HOMUNCULORDS) *and "bad guys" (the* MUTANIGIANS). *the* HOMUNCULORDS *themselves, led by the warrior known as* GUILOTEETH, *were a rebel team of diminutive monster-men, each representing different tribes that had been either wiped out or enslaved by the* MUTANIGIANS; *a trio of much larger monsters who believe themselves to be the last living descendants of the ancient god-beasts who first laid claim to their home world of* UNDERUS; *a once thriving "meta-society" that has devolved into a "living necropolis" once the* MUTANIGIANS *seized control.*

*while the character dynamics and world-building wasn't too dissimilar to other collections on the toy aisle, the* HOMUNCULORDS *toy line / cartoon / mini-comics seemed to be aimed at boys who might have been gradually aging out of MAGNATE's more "quaint"* DINO-SWORDS *figures, with* HOMUNCULORDS *striking a much more violent, grotesque tone that felt like an only slightly more "kid-friendly" interaction of the EVIL DEAD worshipping splatter cinema and gory post-ALIEN creature features of the day.*

*KIRITSIS' memories are more specifically inclined toward the giant-sized MUTANIGIAN antagonists of the HOMUNCULORDS mythos, as indeed were most children's (and later collectors') attentions with regards to the set. aside from slightly more detail and more horror-show looking armor and masks, the HOMUNCULORDS themselves only veered slightly from the archetypal "heroic" characters that populated the young male fantasy genre, but the MUTANIGIANS resembled something much more twisted, severe, and dark... designs that looks to have been commissioned to an artist collective featuring Zdzisław Beksiński, Pushead, Stanisław Szukalski, and Jeff Whitehead.*

*the three "deluxe size" MUTANIGIAN figures were;*

*LICHENTHROPE: a swamp-dwelling fungal she-wolf, furred with moss and veined with ropey vines.*

*SKABAURUS: a zombified-humanoid mound of scar tissue and open wounds with a hippopotamus skull for a head.*

*RAWZERACK : the overfed leader of the MUTANIGANS; a wild pig's head on the body of a silverback gorilla, fur and skin died orange being dipped in HOMUNCULORD blood, who due to his immobilizing corpulence must climb into a mechanized "brace-frame", built from the skeletons of RAWZERACK s own race, enabling him to move around and augment his depleting strength and less-*

*than-threatening build.*

*the MUTANIGIANS were so much so the talk of toy town that MAGNATE would attempt to outdo the MUTANIGIANS in both detail and size in their DINO-SWORDS line with the nearly four foot high VOLCANUS figure, which ended up backfiring on them, as the price-tag was just too much for parents to shell out on something that would more than likely give their children nightmares as it stood in the corner of their rooms.*

*when a second series of HOMUNCULORDS figures failed to replicate the success of the first series, GAUNTLEAN ceased operations, and the molds for the HOMUNCULORD and MUTANIGAN figures were purchased by MAGNATE, who utilized them for what would end up being the final DINO-SWORDS series; a lazy, spiteful cop-out that satisfied no one and left little behind but cheaply imitated repaints warming the pegs of toy stores across the nation.*

*(note: while the designers claimed to have been inspired by creatures mined from obscure mythologies\*, THE MUTANIGIANS were noted by some to be a bit derivative of adversaries that appeared in ROBOVIOLET KAIJU-MAN; the little-known-in-the-states tokusatsu franchise, starring a cosmic monster-fighting superhero of the same name, who went on to become a regular fixture in the Japanese film, television, anime, manga, toy, and*

*game markets. it has been rumored that* GAUNTLEAN *intended to snag the rights to produce a line of* ROBOVIOLET KAIJU-MAN *toys in the U.S., but no agreement could be reached with the creator* RINAKO FUJIWARA *and primary right's holder* BURUYOKU STUDIOS, *which led to* GAUNTLEAN *creating something of a Frankensteinian action figure line with* HOMUNCULORDS. *this theory has never been explicitly confirmed, although it should be mentioned that around the time* HOMUNCULORDS *was launched,* PANIGAI US#1, *the American division of the Japanese toy company* PANIGAI, *released an action figure of* ROBOVIOLET KAIJU-MAN *himself, a sight to be held as it glittered on the shelves with its chromium blue body paint and reflective silver mask/boots/belt/gloves behind its window box, resembling a palate-swapped version of Lee Falk's* PHANTOM\*\*, *scaled to be at the same height as the* MUTANIGIANS *from* HOMUNCULORDS. *it was not a big hit with kids, seeing as how the figure's only tie-in was an incomprehensible English-dubbed re-edit of the 1970s* ROBOVIOLET KAIJU-MAN *live action series [airing in many markets at either 5 or 6 am Saturdays or Sundays... Channel 11 in NY), and the collector's market for* ROBOVIOLET KAIJU-MAN *has never been big in the states, although it hasn't stopped the* SERENGETI COUP *streaming service from making nearly all of the* ROBOVIOLET KAIJU-MAN *shows and films [both live-action and* *animated] featured on their package as they prepare for the stateside première of* SHIN RVK-MAN, *a "gritty, deconstructionist" take on the normally psychedelic and campy* ROBOVIOLET KAIJU-MAN *property, spearheaded by MINYA TSUZIO [best known for creating* GRUDGE NURSE *and* EVIL HERO SHAW].)

*(\*the designers never clarified which obscure mythological beings they were referring to, but KIRITSIS does indeed know of one entity that maybe could have served as an inspiration. while deep in his studies at THE FRACTURE COMPOUND, KIRITSIS became particularly fixated on the myth of SCAVILKADVRIS; a skulking stalker/scavenger being that existed on the margins of the multiverse during the PROTO-MORDIAL era, before their reign was forever razed by the coupling of LYCANIVVE and JANRUMACH. SCAVILKADVRIS evidently went mad with passion and jealousy over the event, though he remain conflict-averse and opted to remain skirting the outer-most edges and traversing the under-most pits of the multiverse, internally marinating in his rampaging frustrations until the simmer became a scald, releasing his grievances in a storm of swords. since SCAVILKADVRIS has never widely documented, not even in NATASHA STAPPO's exhaustive SCARECROW REVOLT, there is only one artist's rendering available, discovered in two recovered illustrations by SILVO ROTPULE, which some suggest were cover art ideas for the*

*unproduced final novel in* THE GLOOM *series, but this cannot be confirmed. the drawings are little more than sketches, ruined by some kind of water or food damage, but there was text written next to the sketches that retained legibility. it reads as follows;* appearing as a curtain of greying flower petals that when jerked open reveals a monstrously enlarged humanoid skeleton with a globular rodent-featured head... eye holes a segmented bubble-grid like that of massive insect... mouth overwhelmed with machete-length tendrils that crowd over each other to create a denture latticework of ruined crosses that have been broken into pointy approximations of the letters S, V, and K. the flesh over the torso and appendages... which are all the same rail-thin length and width, making the figure resemble a crude homemade doll fashioned out of bean poles... appears to be a moss-thick layer of runny egg contents, where premature hatchlings have been ground up and stirred into the yolk until it has been rendered a drowning victim shade of blue. *of the MUTANIGIANS, it is perhaps SKABAURUS who most closely resembles this description, with a few deviations of course. LICHENTHROPE and RAWZERACK could be slightly more conventionally deranged stand-ins for LYCANIVVE and JANRUMACH, respectively.*)

(**in fact, ROBOVIOLET KAIJU-MAN was created when BURUYOKU STUDIOS failed to obtain the rights to Lee Falk's THE PHANTOM, so they hired manga artist RINAKO FUJIWARA to create* ROBOVIOLET KAIJU-MAN *with specific instructions to remain close to Falk's Phantom design. as for the monsters, they were all original creations from her, having first appeared in her violent horror manga* SADISUTIKKUFINDOGADIAN, *which was later adapted into an ero-guro hentai by NYUNOMARU.*)

mealing. slit-drier halting stalks. blue crash spectrums fizz. sperms harden plush where germ-beds maturate for the benefit of fogging oven lights. separated backs. their curved hollow drapes the bolted divot of a puffed arm. mattress salt phases ripped holes, shredded felts braiding tension. throttled 'til masked in a face unseen. malarial lolling. misting adrenochrome. latex chassis roped in tectonic fissures. crescent hairlines reanimate carrion into geysering daughters. if only these protesters had connections to obscenely wealthy child sex traffickers.

a young woman in a sparse white house puts up her

bare legs on a sofa with no back, wearing a nearly shear black and white vertically striped shirt as if it were a nighty, and reading a worn-out copy of *Laconique* by Simone Vanique.

the exposed parts of her are coated with a beading glisten; a side effect of the summer's dog heart, which even at this late phase of the evening... even with her placement directly below a ceiling fan and behind a large open window... retains its enveloping oppression on the earth. she briefly puts down the book so she can pull up her thick brown hair, which has begun to coil in spitting curls from the obstinate humidity, wiping down the back of her neck on the arm of the couch.

the woman turns to inspect the outer dark of the open window. the night's void has subsumed the neighborhood in a whirring fog. she returns her attention to the evening's chosen reading material. behind the window, the after hour haze begins to swirl, as if a dimensional slip is about to become dilated by forces from a parallel universe. a pair of clawed hands materialize in the flashing vapors, reaching past the window and into the house.

the woman can barely correlate the senses required to process this sudden atmospheric shift before a twin set of gun metal mitts interlock their digits around her soft wet throat. her desperate lunge for the farther side of the couch only serves in pulling the assailant... an ether-wraith whose ambient essence acts as a corroding agent against the concealer of the nighttime's shadow... onto the couch with her.

the assailant's frame is less that of a male than of an angry twelve-year-old's inner self as a pit-fighter construct; a mound a bulging musculature carved to the underflesh and vined with vascular lightning bolts, all either dipped or poured into chromium blue vinyl. the assailant's face is hidden behind a bone-colored leather rapist mask, eyes and mouth a trio of glittering silver Xs, suggesting a second mask under the gimp hood made from a grated mesh.

the assailant once again goes for the woman's burning white throat... its flesh further saturated from the new sweat of sheer panic... and lifts her off the couch, pulling her toward the ceiling, her hair being grazed by the plastic blades of the fan, forecasting either the entanglement of her scalp or the rotator-whacking of her skull. the assailant then slams her back down on the backless sofa, releasing one hand from around her neck to grab at the collar of her overlong static test pattern bar shirt, gripping into it and pulling it down and around, knotting his fist around her scruff, yanking her forward with one hand while pressing down on her neck with the other, scraping his taloned fingernails along the length of her carotids.

smash-cut to the blue of a crashed computer screen. white letters fade into the surface of the blank wall of color.

DAXIS presents:

**BLUE GLOOM**

featuring MONA GRUB and starring THYLACINE as **"S**adis**V**alic**K"**

full clip-serial coming soon.

only on DEEP WEB MACUMBA.

cellphone factory suicide nets. taxidermized possum head adhered to the nub of a butt plug. feel those lips come through that hole. an omni-sexual anti-comedic body horror performance piece from the dilating maw of an art-damaged scorched earth. still can't believe the name "HOBONER" has not been taken.

abundant absence. night lowered bricks to pattern slow-wells. lights in a basket like guillotined cherubs. the sum-total of the outer earth replicates the reassuring interior of a windowless van with a side door that has been airbrushed with tiny red handprints. i shove you down my throat until your face becomes lodged in my mouth.

on the right hand side of the foot of my bed there sits and emaciated simian with a block of ashy coal for a head. it's positioned like a deformed tiki idol of a starvation victim; skeletal-severe arms wrapped around wicker-fragile kneecaps that are being pressed against a papery torso. a quilt of soiled dishrags is draped over the protrusive shoulders like a cloak of gore-damp animal hide, its slack braided around the circumference of a wire halo above the collar. the only parts of the body that move are the hands, which shift in a hazy fade of secret societal code. when i attempt to mirror my fingers with it, i swear i can hear a stream of encouraging grunts from somewhere deep in the bowels of either myself or this thing. when the attempts at dialogue fail to progress beyond the wordless trade of gangland symbolism, i become momentarily overwhelmed by a lapse in frustration control and kick at the thing, which causes a slip-back into the waking iteration of my reality... my underflesh gauzed in a sensate fizz.

*KIRITSIS swears that among his horde of detritus there exists a hardcore X-rated cut of the 1980s horror comedy* LYCIRA: MAITRIESSE OF THE GLOOM, *though it's more than likely a bootleg video edit forgery that compiles scenes from that film with scenes from its pornographic doppelgänger;* MS. ANNE THROPE: MONSTRESS OF THE SHADOW HAREM.

glue water. head by the inch. curls press a spongy bone. parch-bumps train the spitters. direct the wadded lungs. racked in the after-binge. manilla pouch chaffed in a flush of wind. caustic surge wall-bombards drowning abrasions. prolapse javeline golden-black like shifting wicks.

apnea backfire. a pen knife tangle up in chewed-out garter belts. graveled cavities perfume a blitz of bricks. chainsaw mounted to rifle found in police raid. genital trench mouth like reading spit in mold found on a palm tree. blocks of chalk like riot masks clouding tears of the eyes sitting on a net of pencils. i am not depressed; you are depressing.

viperfish feeldoe. malice traps inside a vast plank crack. pill meats cease the licker's call. leaking rat meal, the underside-pall of squirming octopuses press against the translucent mold of an exaggerated human form. there are a total of twenty six letters in SVK.

LONG ISLAND VIDEO 13 NEWS REPORTING: once respected local physician Dr. Hyrum Nudesco is in handcuffs tonight, arrested on multiple charges of child endangerment and possession of a large variety of illegal pornographic materials.

at one time a revered figure in the local medical field, with many of the highest profile families and residents counted among his patients, Dr. Nudesco's practice took a hit when his son Cyrus, after a lifetime of struggling with an undiagnosed mental illness, brutally murdered an elementary school bus driver in front of a class that had been preparing for a field trip. Cyrus was soon after committed to the Iris Thacher Memorial Asylum, due in no small part to Dr. Nudesco's connections with the Dr. Clarence Thacher, the late owner of the controversial facility and son of its namesake.

for a little over a decade (just around the time of the catastrophic inmate uprising at Thacher Memorial, rumored to have been spearheaded by Cyrus himself), Dr. Nudesco has been living in relative exile out of his somewhat sprawling home in Gold Ring Harbor, sporadically emerging from the willful quietude of social isolation for a quick trip to a nearby convenience store for the paper and a coffee, content to have the heat of his family name stomped out to the last ember.

however, a recent social media post from Hawntag resident Liza Monday has once again found the name "Nudesco" the subject of prurient infamy, as the post accuses Dr.

Nudesco of molesting Liza's younger sister Candice when she was only around seven or eight years old, Nudesco having been the Monday family's physician at that time. Candice herself disappeared when she reached age sixteen, the same age as Liza's friend Layla Thacher (no known and/or admitted relation to Dr. Clarence Thacher) when her uniquely mutilated body was found at Limer's Pond nearly thirteen years earlier, an event which many believe to be the entrance point for the intervening years of bizarre violent phenomena that has continued to rock this area into a stasis of decay.

according to Detectives Norglam and Opastop, who arrived at the Nudesco house nearly a month after Liza's post went viral, Dr. Nudesco was "eerily cooperative", and put up no struggle. a search of the premises only turned up two items of interest, each for different reasons than the other;

- a hollowed out see-through life-size female anatomy model that had been filled to capacity with baby squids.

- a DV-R in a dark blue case titled JERK CURTAIN, the name spelled out across a sky-blue background in what looks like puffy refrigerator magnets (also dark blue).

upon viewing the contents of the DV-R, the self-proclaimed hardened detectives, who made it a point to mention that they have firsthand accounts of the absolute worst their jurisdiction has produced, couldn't begin to articulate the images they viewed on the DV-R (or their opinions on them) without collapsing into bitter, hopeless tears.

Dr. Nudesco's bail has been set at $500,000,000.79.

Bermuda widows. secreter's blast radius. a sweeping lash pounces to counter, measured in salt curation propels. it only called for rain in the timber of my aches, surging to a pointed whirl at the isosceles horizon.

the hall goes dark. Thou's cover of "Prayer to God" by Shellac begins to rumble through the sound system. a mutant shadow materializes from a dense ether of twisting blue-grey smoke, hooded and robed in a sheet of corrugated iron that's patterned with rust like contents of dried-wound. the figure lowers to the ground, walking forward on gloved fingertips. the figure arches up, revealing a face like a ruined mannequin, eyes Xed out with duct tape and mouth stitched until it resembled a bulk of crabbed penmanship. a large rune covers the length of the mask's forehead; what looks like a F with an S coiling around the lower half.

"the following contest is scheduled for one fall. crawling to the ring, from the Chalk Heart of Gromorrah..."

a graphic fades into view beneath the broken doll countenance, letters of a name being birthed in the peeling of the haze like gothic architecture phasing back into view after an apocalyptic sandstorm, perfectly timed with the declaration of the unseen ring announcer, who struggles to retain her composure ;

# FRANCO SECT

Sect's predatory animal march does its best to compliment the pulverizing gloom of the sludge-metal walkout. by the time he reaches the ring, it is so fogged with icy chrome vapor that when he stands upright, it looks as if he is emerging from a industrial hot spring.

when the lights come up, Sect's opponent... a ham-and-egger named "Holden Manglor", already a fixture among the cans of Savage Brutality Wrestling... appears utterly perplexed; like when a bragadocious poser is confronted by the reality of the power and violence they pretended to yield and perpetrate.

Sect removes the mottled duster, which doesn't so much drop off his large shoulders as it does slough off like gore-sodden flesh, followed by removing the crypto-defaced mannequin head. the face beneath the mannequin head is covered in similar markings, only more smeared and dense, not to mention jagged from being drawn over clusters of psoriasis. Sect's torso and arms are also covered in repetitions of the rune, as well as innumerable other unusual phrases and images. his in-ring ensemble is completed by a pair of form-hugging dark grey slacks, shiny brown driver gloves, and rust-colored leather boots.

the bell rings. Sect makes short work of Manglor, the action deliberate in its messiness and overwhelming in its dark intensity... a release of accumulated frustrations expressed through the canvas offered by performative combat. by the time Sect hits his finisher; the end result of splicing a DDT and a scoop-slam he calls "the Atrocity Conduit", the crowd begins to relent in their enthusiasm and starts to concern themselves with the understanding that maybe Sect (and maybe perhaps themselves) should perhaps process their grief through healthier means.

*KIRITSIS finds himself once more in the grips of another bout of randomly occurring anxious frustration... a sort of bowel-churning hum of post-traumatic stress where the accumulated embarrassments of the stalking past, the overwhelming present, and the plausible future propel their wraiths in a chain surge of flickering barrages. being the accommodating shoulder-to-cry-on never worked... being the terminally negative anti-social contrarian misanthrope never worked... any attempt to situate himself within the womb-like comfort of those who are in communion with his peculiarities never worked... all attempts at interaction marked by the inevitable denouement of a complete backfire... the resultant state of existence always circling the coffin-worm drain toward the cascading alienation where his multiplying shadow-sides teem with greasy knives locked tight between their bile-varnished lips.*

lava tube residency. revolving ticks fabricate meat cuts. serial killers fuck a Nazi's dead pussy with the petrified fecal matter of a newborn burn victim smeared up inside the soak-holes of their raping cocks. opposite bat jaundice in the blue parts. destitute and corpulent. living parents he prays to have shot. the emblem stretched across his asshole.

*"Branded" by Rose Tattoo sits at the very top of KIRITSIS' socially isolated rage killer cringe dance playlist.*

{VOID}

back lashes healed into a rain of faces like skulls pressing through a wall of DNA clag. burn ward embroidery. scar tissue worn as a veil. gelatin webbing in stars across jerkied curtains. pulling teeth out of cement with tweezers in the dark.

*while perusing through the outdoor flea market at the Moebrell train station, KIRITSIS noticed several antique baby dolls that were caked in mold and dirt. they reminded him of photos taken of children pulled from the rubble and wreckage of any number of the more consistently war-torn areas of the globe.*

powdered windows. delinquent spermatozoa. the pink-shocked jaundice backwash of twenty six orbital lacerations dried to a sticky purple on the deep blue sleeves, smearing bruise-dye on reflective lens, and begriming a pair of long chrome shards in beauty mark clusters. when the blades are forced to kiss their points, they resembled a star-packed night sky reversed by a nuclear blast and viewed through a slit in the blind.

LONG ISLAND VIDEO 13 NEWS REPORTING: thirteen young men are in critical condition after a ballistic knife attack at the Sky Inside Motel in Shareboy, which was hosting an event organized by controversial PUA guru Seamus Gintload.

one of the victims, Fretpore native Mack Pereleti, was able to describe the assailant to a police sketch artist; likely a male, face wrapped in egg-white bandages, blue-tinted mirror-lensed goggles over the eyes, silver tape in an X across the face. the assailant was wearing grey pants, brown gloves, shiny black leather shoes, and a navy blue field jacket covered with patches of an emblem that looked like the letters S, V, and K pushed together into a single shape.

Detectives Norglam and Opastop have confirmed to reporters that there was a near fifty page type-written note left at the scene of the crime, but have yet to reveal any details of its contents to the public, only describing the tone of the letter as "meanderingly splenetic".

more as the story develops.

"so last night while watching TV i flipped from *Lovecraft Country* to the Republican National Convention, and i gotta tell ya, after watching a series brain melting non-sequiturs culminate in a ghoulish overkill of apocalyptic spectacle whose morose

{VOID}

comedy value i'm still not sure is entirely intentional, it felt good to switch back to *Lovecraft Country*."

- Whillice Rison, from the *SpaminKiller* newsletter.

cartilage stiletto. pioneering fatality rate. cuspid gnashing ingrown mound. party clown sex doll boiled in a glycerin trough. asphalt bidet. start out on belly. pull up to lay cracks. globular column distends in syruped blood. hanging lead grew fat to stir clean pulping insolence. ventilate libidinal simmering that threatens to shadow faculties in a permanent mushroom cloud of radioactive overcast. unloading nut couldn't foresee the coming pink.

*KIRTISIS spent much of the day decompressing by watching the music videos and concert footage of SYRIN VEDA K; the mixed genre singer/dancer who seamlessly blends the cryptic visuals/lyrics of the more bizarre strands of underground metal and art with the ultra-raunchy theatrics of any number of Dionysian divas in hip hop.*

*SYRIN VEDA K's latest track, "Gluteus Necrosis", is of particular interest to KIRITSIS, as the video was shot on location at TATTERDEMALION, and featured many of the club's regular performers and patrons, including blink-and-you'll-miss-it-but-you'll-cum-anyway cameos from PIXY DEVILLE and VIVIAN GAUNTLEAN,*

*the story line of the video see SYRIN VEDA K touring*

*the Masochistian Suites of TATTERDEMALION, bearing witness to aktions that range from amorous to humorous, while she is stalked and fondled by masked men and women in blue. SYRIN VEDA K's outfit in the video is one for the ages; an air tight cobra-hooded sleeveless blue nylon body stocking, glistening underflesh revealed by large claw marks, backless down to base of her spine, offering a peek of her defining feature. as for the front, the neckline plunges to a point at the top of her mound, cut to form the letters S V K. her eyes are hidden behind reflective blue cop glasses, and three Xs have been drawn in grey over her blue lips. dark brown half-gloves with jointed silver talons and matching thigh high stiletto boots complete the attire.*

*SYRIN VEDA K pantomimes the song, its music a collision of warped binurals and sharp, dark synth pop, with elevating carnal menace; the automatically written verses rapped in an hauntingly erotic ASMR (stand-out lyrics; "My Throat is a Gender-Neutral Bathroom"), while the chorus booms with an uncharacteristic hardcore scream of "THEY EAT MY ASS UNTIL MY ASS EATS THEM", which causes both her and the extras to explode in a frenzy of unrestrained intensity, all of them bathed in a film projection of strobing imagery culled from porno films, many of which KIRITSIS recognizes as being sourced from deep cut visions of the Perpetually Consuming Passions video library.*

*the photography of the video seems heavily influenced by the work of HANS KLATE, particularly his unfinished CLEAN HOLES photo/video series, which he began sometime before his disappearance. the CLEAN HOLES series was also positioned to be the breakthrough for LILI VIOLBLOOM; a pretentiously prickly alt-fetish model who had been slowly gaining steam on the backend of the late 00s brief flirtation with cyber-goth fashion and Lolita-adjacent ruined youth beauty standards.*

*when KLATE vanished, LILI VIOLBLOOM went on a splenetic viral tantrum that she somehow synchronized across all of her social media platforms. when the more "intrepid" among her pasture of pervert patrons checked the time stamps on each post and saw they all matched, they wondered how that could be. it didn't take much further prodding for the ruse to be uncovered; LILI VIOLBLOOM had paid content providers running her social media accounts, who would pretend to be her.*

*the discovery led down a rabbit hole of deceit, eventually culminating in the revelation that "LILI VIOLBLOOM" didn't actually exist. the model in the photographs was LYNETTE CAILADRI ; a Long Island runaway who had been reported missing in the mid-00s. at the aggrieved insistence of her much older boyfriend GILES MEWLPYS, she found herself nudged into the universe of fetish modeling, which was in the midst of a pin-up revival, marrying those* traditions with mild punk/metal/industrial culture aesthetics and a light touch of BDSM.

CAILADRI's first photoset under the name LILI VIOLBLOOM was titled "Tunnel Nun". in the set, she is depicted as having been hanged by a nun's habit from the roof of a filth-encrusted tunnel, simulated blood, spit, and mud spiraling down her arms and legs, making them look like neopalitan candy canes. from her slack mouth there is a large grub on her tongue; a puffed communion wafer choking hazard.

it was this set; an "homage" to the murder scene of LAYLA THACHER, that saw LILI VIOLBLOOM banned from the popular SCARREDVIXENS website, but the controversy served as a beacon for those who sought for more a challenging branch to the burgeoning "alt-porn" scene, which was already approaching saturation (and stagnation).

the LILI VIOLBLOOM brand was now up and running. in addition to her photosets, where she drew from Japanese erotica, European surrealism, and American Pornography from its "Golden Age", a few interviews were given, where she came across as a wise-beyond-her-years expert on seemingly all kinds of subcultures, ranging from vintage S&M art to contemporary power electronics, always making sure to connect herself to the bigger names of this "loli-goth" moment by insulting them viciously (and often without being prompted to mention them). the desired *intention seemed to be manufacturing feuds with bigger names (AEVEA WITHIN was an oft-cited target for VIOLBLOOM's confusingly sex-negative vitriolic articulations), but none of these individuals took the bait, making VIOLBLOOM appear as part over-eager contrarian, part dangerously needy stalker.*

*the photographers who worked with "LILI VIOLBLOOM" (LYNETTE CAILADRI ) were taken aback by the brutal savagery of her online presence, as on the set of a shoot she would be invariably polite, agreeable, even a bit silly and prankish. as it turned out, LYNETTE CAILADRI herself didn't even handle the interviews, which were all done by email. to this day, no one has been able to figure out who wrote these responses, or who handled her social media presence in general.*

*once the jig was up, LYNETTE CAILADRI went into seclusion, and the LILI VIOLBLOOM brand went with her; a curio among the detritus of terminally fleeting trends.*

digital bomb cloud the color of pizza cheese. blurred waking eyeline scan is jolted by the presence of an egg-shaped woman in my sewer main domicile. she introduces herself as "Lia DeFesisc". she says she's looking for her roommate. his name is "Mr. Nozog". she had heard somewhere that he had come through here. maybe i saw him? he's very skinny and probably nude except for a cape of lavender dishrags and a box of ash he wears over his head. he only responds verbally to a rapid motion of the hands.

"sounds like someone who came to me in a sleep paralysis hallucination."

"sHyEAh... wE GeT ThAt aLoT!"

when Lia DeFesisc talks she puts intense emphasis on random letters, like when you wanna make someone on a comment section looks stupid by TyPInG wHaT THeY sAId lIkE ThIS. Lia Defesisc wears a blue silver kimono, its color matching her hair, which has been pulled tight to the sides of her scalp and braided into a pair of stiff pigtails. the area around her eyes is painted in target practice circles of white, grey, and black, which makes her look like a pre-WW2 era cartoon. when she parts her greyish pink lips, she can't help but flash her heavily braced teeth, which resemble an iron wall weeded in barbwire and decorated with first responder crosses.

"AnYWhooooOOOOooo.... I gOtTa KEeP LOoKiNG. dOn'T Be a StRAnGer DAnGeR!"

Lia DeFesisc floats away on the air like a shark drunk on whale blubber. her laugh is the zombified regurgitate of a child molesting party clown that was conceived, born, and educated at a dixie cult ritual orgy between meth heads and crocodiles.

when summer ends, i will cum buckets.

a figure laconically glides across a desert of lunar-hued powder, a glitching spectral expansion of the ruined world they find themselves scouring at the midnight stroke. their body is cloaked in a duster the same shade of blue as the Mariana Trench, face obscured behind a gas mask that resembles the boiled-clean skull of an abnormally large possum, which protrudes from beneath broadbrimmed grey hat. this figure, known among the whispered lore of the forgotten as SUB-CROSSER, can usually be seen dragging behind them a body bag connected to a rope of braided chainmail. the body bag is used for storage of items they discover and for sleep purposes.

- from pg. 1313 of *SKARSGROTH: SPIDER'S VEGETATION* by S. Delancey Allprick (book 4 in sub-series 9 of *THE WRATHGUILD TOMES*)

puritan backdoor. Aghori Sadhu instructional videos. knuckles slashed on pelvic mesh. feeling as if i've been reliving middle school for the last four years. looking on simmering alienation as longtime friends and members of your own family almost gleefully renew their most egregious and capricious impulses from those thoughtlessly vicious schoolyard days. impotent hubris. premature curmudgeons. zany smart-ass pranksters. bottom feeding contrarian maggots. a wearying deference to vindictive personal attacks. needlessly snarky and terminally incredulous. overwhelmed by greed, entitlement, cynicism, and bile. vulgar, chaotic appeals to the most deplorable of the low. pretending to care about others, but only as generalized abstractions.

the right and left... the alt and the hard... their modus operandi are in exact alignment; frustrate the exploited proletariat to the point of deeply pessimistic spiritual exhaustion, then scavenge the carrion fields for anyone willing to smother what remains of their pulverized identity for the sake of the most vaguely defined of "greater goods". rather than constructive approaches of even mournful reflection, they opt instead to take superior delight in their cut-throat nihilistic sadism being validated by the bowel-eroding awfulness of the world's events.

among the multitude of reasons that led us to this seemingly insurmountable impasse were asshole fake idiots who say things like "ThEy'Re AlL eQuALLy bAd!"; incoherent maladapted role-playing social rejects... either menstruating platitudes about children they'll never see being drone-striked in countries they can't name or hocking ream upon ream of splenetic hyperbole about their theoretical darlings being snatched off the pristine any town streets by parademonic globalist predators, who will pimp them out to obscenely wealthy shadow-pedophiles who perform sacrificial rites of devotion to an animal-faced false god while clad in baby blood splattered lizard-skin clown robes.

and checking social media? checking social media is like having unwillingly wandered into a town square lynch mob gauntlet and getting doused to the back of your eyeholes with a work week accumulation of blood/piss/shit/puke cocktails... the discourses overwhelmed by unbearably miserable full-body skin tags who can't stand to go a full thirteen hours without dropping some "hot takes"... you do know of "hot takes", correct? those intellect-negative rectum shedding's of maliciously terse insta-observation that serve no purpose beyond making others feel like they should've have been swallowed because they have the temerity to allow themselves the privileged luxury of actually liking something?

i know there will always be people like this; callous ambulance chasers, shameless tabloid ghouls, and sneering failed comedians... whose own cavernous lack of imaginative speculation will cause them to lean into self-nullifying codependency on impulsively negative commentary and resentfully jealous deconstructive critiques of those who can create and/or appreciate content that speaks to places within us that are just a scant few feet deeper than just narcissistically harp on a misguided feedback loop of rawboned grievances.

so i brumate... coiling sharp and tight into my private

worlds... renewing my most egregious and capricious impulses from a youth spent marinating the lash in a steady flow of creamery venom.... bottling it up until i succumb to sepsis from a rupturing ulcer.

*KIRITSIS mood shifted to the affirmative spectrum when he finally found his copy of the SWORN VIRGIN / COLLATERAL PENANCE split 7' and his framed poster of* MANHATCHET, *Hector Bellone's vicious late 70s/early 80s NYC based stalker/slasher film, where the villain (who is named "GHOST APPLE" in the credits) is standing before a midnight blue sky, wearing a dirty white ski-mask and a buttoned-up dark denim jacket. on the poster, GHOST APPLE is drawn as an ax wielding giant towering behind the Chrysler Building, which is positioned just below his waistline to give potential viewers an idea of the priapic savagery awaiting them.*

when i was in second grade, the class was assigned to write their own Halloween story. i had just read *the Witches* by Roald Dahl, and i would frequently imagine myself a willing subordinate to the hairless child-hating crones of the story... offering up mean classmates and neighborhood children to them in exchange for a place in their world. so for the assignment, i wrote a nasty piece of wish fulfillment about a little boy who helps a local witch by luring his schoolyard peers into her house, which is built from the broken toys of the children she captures. once the little darlings are ensnared, the witch would then use magic to turn the children into small pigs, which she would then feed to her pet sea monsters. i remember describing the witch as resembling Carol Kane because i thought she was the prettiest lady in the world who was also weird and kinda scary.

*KIRITSIS caught an infomercial for the PANTHEON SCHOOL OF EXTREME ALTRUISM (PSEA); an amalgam of a teenage superhero academy, a strip mall karate dojo, a sketchy youth outreach center, and a clown college. the PSEA was opened by THE PANTHEON; a "real life superhero" team that was founded by the table scraps left behind after the rampage period of "THE CAPE KILLER".*

*the pickings for this team occupied the sub-tier of the RLSH community;*

*- OVERCOMER: christian over toned alpha of the group.*

*- WOLF WARRIOR: a militaristic police-themed vigilante whose superpower is evidently not detecting contradictions.*

*- DOLL DRUMS: a moody goth girl with a look that could be described as "Victorian futurist".*

*- BOONDOGGLE: a silly, irreverent, tiresomely "wacky" type.*

*- RED MIRAGE: a hyper-conspiratorial moral objectivist with a domino-masked gravel throated*

*private eye aesthetic and a singularly tense "protests-too-much" focus on perceived child sex crimes among liberal elites.*

*- GLASS BLOWER: a "super-chanteuse" with a reported 13 octave range.*

*- WARPZONE: the one that can run really fast. formerly the sidekick / love interest of DING DONG DITCH, who was chopped in half by "the Cape Killer".*

*hoping to swell their ranks; THE PANTHEON decided to open the PSEA with the outsized presumption that there would be lines around the block of willing recruits. turnouts must be low, as made clear by the ceaseless walking desperation of the PSEA infomercial. heavy on redundant platitudes, demonstrably coached testimonials, clumsily staged demonstrations, and the broad promise of unexiting, unearned wish fulfillment. in those ways, one can't accuse the advertisement of not being firmly planted in the outmoded traditions of the superhero genre; both the imagined and "real world" iterations of that milieu....*

....no matter how much "weightier" it presents itself to be, the superhero paradigm still depends on the kind of magical thinking that undergirds those post-WWII era body builder ads; where a dweebish beanpole gets embarrassed on the beach by some conventionally handsome jock-ass in front of several pretty ladies, afterward seeking to achieve mythical physical betterment to ensure it never happens again.

the irony is that, more often than not, the newly minted meta-man seeks placement among those sand-kicking bullies and bathing beauty chuckle-monsters who without prior provocation sought him out for humiliation and ridicule, making him pivot his rage inward until his life is a tactile nightmarescape of insecurity, doubt, resentment, and loathing... in effect recirculating his new found power back to those over-influential spite hordes who already possess more power than they know what to do with.

tongue canal. secret algorithms. carbonated flesh chain. unbalanced pettiness. chokehold elbows like tenting neck-sacks made into points by iron rods that impale the stressing brainstems from behind their phase-shifting skins. cutting grease smokes moss when broken by pipe. rape this cunt with a faggot of hair pins.

stripped woman splayed open on an anvil the size and length of an operating slab. long ropes are tied around her ankles, positioned to reach behind her head, arching her ass off the lead of the anvil, spreading her wide enough for her clenching cunt to gasp like the mouth of a beached mackerel.

the other ends of the ropes are wrapped around triangular fixtures that have been bolted into the slat-fenced walls directly behind her. her arms are zip-tied together at the wrists. a length of motorcycle chain... pulled through an oxen nose ring that has been nailed to the floor under her head... has been looped around the zip-tie, locked into a hoop with a padlock.

crack of a narrow lash, emerging off frame as to render it sentient... its movement independent of a dominant's instigation. the echo of a cord-thin whip touching down on the sweet meat reverberates like crackling flames in a concert hall crematorium. the caustic thrashing of the woman's ass continues until the bruises begin to bead with cherry syrup condensation, her carotid arteries threatening to erupt out of her neck to hiss and flail like burning serpents.

the lash relents. a large taloned hand, clothed to the bone in cobalt latex, smears the blood forming on the ass, rubbing it over the latex until it's a gleaming drip of chromium purple. the shiny violet claws reaches downward to cup a sizable erection, condomed to the throbbing veins inside the waist appendage attached to the cobalt body suit. the claws lubricate the cock with the blood from the wounds of the ass, dyeing the head a shaft their same gradiation of bruise.

the man in the cobalt body suit is bulky but cut, face hooded in a white gimp mask with a crooked X-shaped zipper-mouth. he circles behind the woman on the anvil, until his plasma-lacquered cock is grazing across her throat. the man slams down his gloved, taloned hands on both sides of the woman's ear, pushing himself up so his knees are resting on the rim of the anvil. the man crawls like a stalking jungle predator of rare origin over the woman's torso, trailing the tip of his cock down her sternum, stopping when his rape-head gets an inch out of reach of her bare ruined cunt.

the man gets on his feet, standing over the woman on the anvil, forming a blood-dripping archway over her body. the man drops his hands down on the floor below her ass, positioned is DNA coated cock against the puckering rim of her asshole. the man drives his cock, lubricated with her blood, directly into her asshole, slamming down and grinding forward and back in violent machine rhythms.

the noises emanating from deep within the ceaselessly pounded guts of the woman on the anvil are devoid of apt comparison. they are beyond all confirmed gender. beyond all known species. beyond any registers of either pleasure or pain.

they are the hottest fucking thing i have ever heard. Daxis has really taken it up a notch with this *BLUE GLOOM* series. I'll have to see if this Mona Grub girl has been in anything else. and this "SadisValiK" character is something i've never seen in porn before, yet feels so intimately familiar to me.

carrion chimera. tensions whipsaw from grenade sprint to obelisk bloat. elephantine thumbs coax petrified gas through a pinpricked hayseed. gloved bone kneads a strip of gills the organ-braid thwacked along the pig.

Joseph Merrick fashions a Hellboy cosplay by utilizing the liquid giblet interior of a radiator-gutted deer carcass. miniature flag impaled through skull as if it were the cratered surface of a claimed moon.

....the clothesline snapped from the pressure of the ear canal... head plummeting toward the concrete brokering the tenements... the ends of the twine joining into a ring from the rapid spiral of the drop.... orbiting the slate-blank face like the ring of a planet that has been unceremoniously dropped from the cradling vacuum of soldering black infinity....

- from *Laconique* by Simone Vanique (translated from French by Ghislaine Nudesco for Villation Books)

extrapolated vulnerabilities. cowed fetal stress in the gutter avian maw. internalized turmoil made manifest in combs of shrapnel. pipe seed. whimpering buckles. itchy baton. wet ripping's amped through a thousand yard daisy chain of riot dispersal megaphones.

grievance accumulation. opinionated hit-pieces land across the eyes and ears like acid thrown from a jar, to be shock-followed by the attacker's incessant spittle-flecked line of questioning about the reasons why you've allowed the launched corrosive to reshape

{VOID}

the molecular structure of your dermal countenance.

a film of spherical mirrored rainbows machine-gunned to dampening ganglia by the sheets of star that tour its lines. if soon you woke with the visions i hold at present, i would have to conclude that their opposite is true.

whether a novelistically profane pop-culture savvy alpha-male cool jerk or a tightly wound over-inhibited nebbish loser, all will be welcomed home by a waiting volcano with guillotines for teeth.

*KIRITSIS recalls his first date with PIXY DEVILLE. it was at the Celluloid Museum House in Nothtingun, a midnight showing of* SUCCUBAPHAGUS; *the insanely lurid Mexican splatter film from writer/director KALYAN SILVASCARAS, adapting from his own "performance instillation" for his theater group THE EXILE CLINIC, who combined mythos from obscure Spanish folklore with the excessive libidinal brutality of fringe European creative enclaves.*

SUCCUBAPHAGUS *stars RACINA MOLIV\* as CONTESSA DEIDREUHM; a blood fetishizing black magic practioneer who has been cast out from all of the most depraved witch cults in the world for being too angrily radical, gleefully violent, unwaveringly extreme, and amorously liberated. DEIDREUHM eventually takes up residence within the labyrinthian confines of a condemned asylum for the criminally* *insane, the patients left behind as skeletons.*

*growing more deranged by the day due to social isolation and deep boredom, DEIDREUHM begins to venture further up the road, alluring wayward travelers with hypnotic suggestions into her decaying complex, where they are grindingly ushered through a chaos gauntlet of flash-bang hallucinations, screaming hate-fucks, and being forced to bear witness to their own meticulous butchery, remaining bleakly aware as their tender parts are chewed up and gulped down with tensing grace of a rupturing orgasm.*

*PIXY DEVILLE had just dyed her hair cherry-soda red. she spent much of the screening near unconscious on KIRITSIS's lap, as she had just gotten off from a pretty busy shift tending the coffee bar at Sedgewick's. KIRITSIS couldn't help but become mildly irritated by her inability to stay awake, as he was fairly anxious to share his favoritism for the work of THE EXILE CLINIC with someone who he felt would understand and appreciate their contributions, as PIXY DEVILLE herself scopes comparable terrain with her performances, writings, and general tastes... but the balm for soothing that stubborn itch lay north of PIX's spine, filling out a pair Black Lodge tile pattern leggings to the point of appearing painted on the ass.*

*KIRITSIS's eyes narrowed before the screen while his*

*right hand clasped on PIX's ass, the feel of the leggings' material overwhelmed by the considerable heft its undermeat. an internal chorus of urgent pleading to spank her began to bombard the percolating neurons, holding tempered focus hostage, until KIRITSIS could no longer maintain the decorative composure of a dating scene avatar.*

*one crisp slap briefly lifted the right cheek up by its cleft fails to register with the scant audience that is currently being marinated in a barrage of surround sound hack-crackle and gut munching. PIX jumps up with the kind of gasp that's normally elicited from the sudden fall of a dinner plate, but quickly falls back into nocturnal stasis... but not before acknowledging the fresh audacity of her date with a wink response.*

*(\*= RACINA MOLIV was also mesmerizingly unhinged as "Sorella Destino"; the skeleton-faced goldmine dwelling doomsday nun of Vincenzo Scappeli's spaghetti western experiment* 13 ROPES DRAW BLOOD ON THE PLAIN, *which introduced audiences to "Hangler", the noose-dragging anti-hero played by Alphonse Garehti. the character of "Hangler" would subsequently be featured in just over a dozen other films from other directors in the genre [in both official and unofficial capacities], out-appearing Scappeli's other creation; "Greasetrap" of the SOW franchise, by three films (though "Greasetrap" far outranks "Hangler" in the departments of cheesy merchandise, ill-advised video*

*game tie-ins [now a downloadable character in* VIOLENT SKUM 13*], and comic book crossovers [the less said about the amateur malpractice that was* THE LIVING GRAVE / GREASETRAP: APPROVAL WOUNDS, *the better] , but that's a discussion for another time.)*

LONG ISLAND VIDEO 13 NEWS REPORTING: controversial right wing firebrand LARSON CUTREK, host of the "WHIPSAW" podcast and TV program, was rushed to the hospital early this afternoon, after receiving a package in the mail that was evidently filled with a little over a dozen capsules of rodenticide, which were somehow rigged to an explosive device that was triggered to detonate upon opening of its delivery. details on CUTREK's condition are scarce, but sources have suggested that he may have suffered eye trauma due to powder burns.

when inquiries about how this poison-bomb failed to arouse suspicion, those same sources told reporters that the package appeared to resemble one from a medical or magazine delivery service, one which CUTREK could have been a regular subscriber to.

after inspecting the charred remains of the packing materials, all that could be recovered was a scrap of blue carboard, its edges singed to grey ash, the word "JERK CURTAIN" written in white-out.

this attack coincides with the anniversary of an event that happened roughly a year ago, when Republican Senator (and frequent WHIPSAW guest) BERTRAM MEWLPYS was the victim of a similar attack, to which he has yet to fully recover.

more as this story develops.

horned breasts. a dragging rear braid teeth-slides have gored sloughs to the pit-grist that gilded their cunts. branded a new breed of provocateur due to their youth, tele genesis, and entry-level know-how with regards to navigating internet platforms as to better manipulate content with the desire to rapidly generate false pop-controversies when the viewpoints they expunge and exploit are no more than the obstinate rancor of 1970s arch-conservatives... reductionist perspectives that have been regurgitated so many times that what emerges is no more than thin white bile... only recontextualized through the memetic prism of hot takes and shit posts, circumventing their rejection from a more substantial cultural milieu by attaching themselves to the content's resultant commentary... moralistic sound 'n fury leech-sponging that once isolated from its bulldozer oration and softcore white nationalist rhetoric can be trimmed, boiled, and cleaned into "what would gam gam and pop pop think?".

spectral reflection in nightshade plexiglass. bandaged outline fading into the beaded sparkles of post-combustion galactic catastrophe. turning away from the door. any cosmic speculations are smash-eroded by the encroaching banality of toast-colored public office aesthetics, their shameful inoffensiveness only slightly dulled by framed mock comic book covers; one for each of the proprietors of this clearly struggling enterprise... one last stab at prolonging cultural relevancy for their good guy/bad buy morals and costume jewelry vigilantism.

"excuse me. i'm sorry but the PSEA is closed for the day. if want to apply for the program you have to make an appoi.."

brown leather glove clasps the gold-lipped mouth before it can sluice with any further performative warmth. dressed like a torch singer from a city that floats among the clouds. rattling tip of long knife breathes on widened left eye. sleeveless arms swat at dark blue field jacket, smearing the still-fresh white out that was used to scrawl the rune that repeated into a series that oscillates in detail and size. attempts to puncture skin under the glove with high octave screams, which are pushed back down to her lungs, their ballooning meat slipping through the grates of the rib cage. another push cracks the back of her skull against the large framed poster of the Pantheon all together, now decorated with deep red pin hammer blow webbing just over the crotch of their leader; a bipedal white cross cloaked in lavender and gold.

now to groggy to struggle, she can be lead down the wall to slump on the floor, involuntarily compliant with the rope-binding of her ankles and wrists. when her head briefly snapped forward after being smashed into the poster, her left eye must have grazed the breathing knife, as there is an ever flowing stream of pus-trimmed orbital fluid going down her cheek like a snotty, unbroken teardrop.

clutch the remaining eleven ropes and head toward the back of the academy or dojo or whatever these "extreme altruists" are calling this monument to desperate nostalgia. i'm put off to find that this "superhero headquarters" is little more than a games room... a toy-strewn suburban den where children are free to indulge their inner howling mongoloid by loudly talking over each other, restlessly jumping from action figures to video games to movie watching... making exaggerated if not outright fraudulent claims about playground spats and secret bleacher relationships... while the adults pretty much do more of the same, albeit with a much larger territory to take in.

the one dressed like a private dick in Dick Tracy villain red makes the first move, stepping over a woman in an ornate runner's outfit and a lanky guy in an atomic yellow body stocking with some "wacky" phrases and pictures all over it, who are in the middle of playing a a modernized version of the early 90s arcade game *VIOLENT SKUM\*;* a splatter-influences side-scrolling brawler about a quartet of slasher villains chopping their way through and Eldritch horror nightmarescape.

"oh hey man sorry we're closed for the night. guys isn't Glass Blower out front? right... yeah she should've told you... but you may have something going here."

Dog Boner still hasn't noticed the long knife or the bulk of ropes, but the bummed-out looking one wearing a crescent-shaped half-mask of a broken doll and a copper-laced Victorian era black dress has picked up on it.

"Red., you don't see the fucki.."

wadded thwack upon traumatized pig. room startles itself out of malaise. spray-pattern on grey slacks rendered root-cellar brown. blade locking target on lean jaundice bendy figure, who at some point has used a marker to draw a face of shock on his lemon candy drop skull. fistful of rope raised shortly after. squirrel-jerking head toward the track meat and the drummed-broken doll.

"tie them. one rope for the ankles. one rope for the wrists. then i'll do you. try nothing."

he complies. they comply. as i'm tying up Lemon Bean, two more enter behind me. a bit larger, but not by much. there's a militarized police officer wearing a wolf-skull mask that's been painted in stripes of black, white, and blue. beside him is the bipedal white cross from the poster in the reception area, who is carrying the torch singer like someone who was a bit to overzealous on their honeymoon night.

"what's going on? who are you?"

i never got that far ahead. i look down at the rune drawn across the surface of the field jacket, and it finally makes a bit of sense.

"...svihck..."

the wolf-pig reaches for a baton that's dangling from his wrestling-championship sized belt. the long knife gets closer the throat of Lemon Bean. wolf-pig halts.

"you. put her down against the wall. take those two ropes and tie up his ankles and wrists. then i'll do you.

try nothing."

he complies. they comply.

"all of you roll onto your bellies if you haven't already. then look forward. then keep looking forward. then don't stop looking forward. whoever breaks will get the thirteenth rope."

they comply, save for the torch singer, who i have to manually drag into this circle of caterpillars. they are all staring into each other... through each other... through the wall to outside... through the outside to the void... through the void to the.

the hackings break the flesh over the spine, the pieces of column peaking like bleached rocks in rain-saturated mud. brown glove pushes past the gore to clench their digits into the curving bone, yanking at it until it juts out like the handle of a suitcase.

the wolf-pig is the first to break, burying his smeared-flag head into the gym mats. the loop of the thirteenth rope goes around his neck, its slack tossed over a nearby pull up bar, where it is to be pulled until the feet halt their wag... but not before he bears witness to the creases in their skin becoming unfolded by the razored lurch of a breath-greased shard.

*(\*= VIOLENT SKUM was released by BURUYOKU STUDIOS, featuring designs from ROBOVIOLET KAIJU-MAN creator RINAKO FUJIWARA. a spin-*

*off of their cult-favorite fighting game* ASYLUM THRASHERS, VIOLENT SKUM *has the four boss fighters of* ASYLUM THRASHERS; *RUDY KUDLOW, SKINCOAT, MICHELLE MEMBERS, and KATIE KIDDO (exaggerated stand-ins for Freddy Krueger, Leatherface, Michael Meyers, and Chucky [and in the case of the last two, gender-swapped]) take center stage, this time out as playable characters. having been defeated in* ASYLUM THRASHERS, *the gruesome quartet of morose savages are sent to a hellish netherworld as punishment, where they must move through 13 worlds teeming with fanatical cultists, cosmic monstrosities, the MORITURIANS (stand-ins for the Deadites from* Evil Dead), *and the SENSECTISTS (stand-ins for the Cenobites of* Hellraiser), *who lord over a burning universe that is not too dissimilar from FUJIWARA's own relentlessly bizarre and graphic* SADISUTIKKUFINDOGADIAN *manga.)*

LONG ISLAND VIDEO 13 NEWS REPORTING: the newly opened Pantheon School for Extreme Altruism became the site of a grisly, almost ritualistic mass murder late last evening.

Detectives Norglam and Opastop have confirmed to this as that the victims were indeed members of "The Pantheon"' the real-life superhero team who opened the facility in the hopes of training a new generation of superheroes, their ranks depleted after the "Cape Killer" slayings a few years back, murders which are heavily echoed in this most recent attack on their community.

only one member of the Pantheon was left alive, "Doll Drums", who provided a detailed description of the assailant; a male, wearing a blue field jacket with the letters SVK written in white on and around the pockets of the coat, grey slacks, brown gloves, face wrapped in bandages, duct tape over the mouth in an X, and blue goggles.

this matches the description of the perp at the nearby Sky Inside Motel roughly a month ago, where attendees of a pick-up artist speaking engagement were blinded in a violent knife attack.

detectives were reluctant to tell media outlets the true identities of the Pantheon, out of fear of reprisal directed toward their friends and loved ones, but they were given the all-clear to reveal the secret identity of "Wolf Warrior"; CYRIL GINTLOAD, a former member of the SECTARIAN KARNAGE AXIS (SKA); an accelerationist militia who's propaganda utilizes gruesome imagery and suggestions of infanticide and child sex abuse as a means to smear non-whites as cold demonic super-predators. the fanatical white-power cult achieved no small amount of public attention when it was revealed that the primary architectural framework of the Spamin Administration's immigration policy drew heavy rhetorical influence from *CERULEAN SWAN*; an oppressively ugly illustrated novel published by SKA, which is loaded to the margins with graphic descriptions of an invariably grisly racial dystopia.

more as this story develops.

STEPHEN MILLER GOT COVID FROM BRUSHING HIS TEETH WITH HOPE HICKS' PANTY RESIN.

sycophant canon. stepped lagoon of shifting rain oil. abrasion documents. adult diaper snow angel. bifurcated seed in coats of lensing gelatin. a brick of frozen roach husks pawned as a pandora's box. latex reptiles towel-snap tourniquet mesh, aggravating diabetic ulcers until they percolate with coffin worm breeding stocks. amber alert is the color of your energy.

hairline mandible. mason jars smashed in duvets. parochial carotid wheezes mercury. cattle skull satellites pollinating black jam. stick bug catheter blooms sarin at the joint. eating an asshole perfumed in the smoke of their charbroiled caseworker. your cunt is a bulimic leech.

gloved hooks trace balloon-smooth flesh of an under cheek, gaping charcoal the lamps render yellow, synchronized with the augmented bulging of salt-cracked eyeholes. up-spurting regions leave stain a glittering metropolitan skyline just beneath the arching whisps of sinister brow, the secretive lurch of its endgame provoking a stir of fretting anxious and tensing arousal.

corridors are wheezing from the brackish tattering of rainfall being ushered through rusting gutters, the humidity visualizing the air into a vapor that makes the grey bricks of the wall appear to be dissolving into micro-dustbowls of twirling smoke. a floating white wrench orbits the sleeve-hole of a hooded blue slicker.

limestone cherub dogpile. curling iron potato bugs. bathtub of ice inhaled to the cervix. a row of insect bites like a bubbled suture of staples keeping the scalp from dropping to the floor from the weight of the ecretea-cabled fiber-mats. microwaves stacked up into a pyramid that obstructs the width and length of an emergency exit. a reflective platter of bloody animal hearts in a sea of mother's milk. tentacle-streams of liquid cuts from a skinned distended crane. vaporized pea-soup emits from under the coiling tongue inside its dislocated beak. ball gags of wadded muscle. greedy palms in the back-tier mutilation's laddered gash.

a woman masturbates to orgasm with a severed head being pulled apart by a pair of wild dogs while wearing a habit that looks to be made out of stratified sewer sludge. lip-skin stretches in a snotty web. holding a life-size ceramic leg like a marine at attention. IV bags filled with aborted fetuses. crime scene photos of a woman with sewing needles driven into every inch of her face lying unconscious beside a boy whose head has been bashed open on a cement floor next to a crib full of hot tar and small bones.

animal noise composite. crash-mangled automobile occupies a soft ditch, coarsening the road with glass-cutting junkyard protrusions. a woman crawls from the wreckage like a flow of pus being drained from a jagged cyst, her wounds like that of a body left to molder in a sewer mane; damp and swollen, colored with smears from a water-logged marble notebook.

ghoul soil. drillbit clitorectomy tinnitus. churning swirls of fermented stomach acid beneath pineal skin guards. standing outside of a warped phone booth with syringes between the gaps in my teeth while holding up a sloshing gas canister in front of an overflowing pediatric hospital like i'm John Cusack in *Say Anything.*

*KIRITSIS spent the early evening reacquainting himself with* GASH LADDER, *which has the dubious honor of being one of the first truly "strange" pieces of media he can remember experiencing at the gradually unhinging gateway to what would come to be a unparalleled adolescence.*

GASH LADDER *is an oppressively hallucinogenic film from Australian maverick auteur HECTOR BELLONE, which would serve as a transitional pivot from the milieus of slasher cinema (*MANHATCHET*), animal attack (*BUSH CLAWS), *gonzo vehicular action (*CONVICT STOCK), *and tawdry sexploitation\* (*PROPER KYLIE, *based on the comic strip character from the BLUE ROSE men's magazine) into more personal, experimental terrains (he would follow* GASH LADDER *with the narratively vague but visually sumptuous post-apocalyptic adult fairytale tone poem* WRAITHS OF THE ETHER, GARGOYLES OF THE DUST).

*adapting from S. DELANCEY ALLPRICK's pathologically atmospheric debut novel, the story is nominally about a group of troubled teenagers and young adults who are committed to a new kind of mental facility, where there are subjected by cryptocratic forces to attack therapy gauntlets, experimental medication cocktails, and sexually invasive obscure religious rituals, with the desired effect being the aggravated jostling of dormant mutations within the subjects, transmogrifying them into shapeshifting paradimensional entities that will serve as the key to bridging the doorways between infinite realities.*

*first being serialized in the seminal weird fiction zine* CUT VISIONS, *Allprick's* GASH LADDER *is a sprawling-ly paranoid sci-fi thriller, with running persistent streaks of ruthless violence, demonic mysticism, and bleak commentary on institutional society's grindingly exploitive maltreatment of those who suffer from immobilizing loops of prolonged psychological duress and engagement with performative bouts of aggressive self-harm, their origins intertwined at the roots of a buried history of childhood sexual abuse. much of the novel reads like testimonials of those who would have had more extended stays at the controversial IRIS THACHER MEMORIAL ASYLUM, Allprick cited as a point of research for his narrative, though he stopped short of saying whether or not he had more first-hand experience with that facility... although he did relent to an admission of having an older sibling who witnessed a gathering of the CYSYSTISM society, which also served as grist for the mills of the book's universe.*

*Bellone's movie adaptation of* GASH LADDER *does hew respectfully close to the provocative content of the source novel, though due to in part to restraints in both the available budget and the special effects of the day, much of the film's imagery is not quite as explicitly rendered as in Allprick's writing. Bellone makes up for this in spades with tactile cinematography, inventively jarring camera work, a proto-power electronic soundtrack from FURIO VALACHI (best known for scoring the pictures of VINCENZO SCAPPELLI) and guttural performances yanked from the bowels of the cast, particularly RACINA MOLIV in the crucial role of "PATTI LEVOURS"; the incidental antagonist of the story.*

*catching the film on Channel 11's "Blue Market Block" when he was hovering around nine or ten years old began to stir something buried deep within the muddy psyche of KIRITSIS. finding a copy of novel among the detritus of THE FRACTURE COMPOUND further expanded this cerebral plume, blotting his amygdala until it existed solely in a roiling state of restless ferox.*

*(\*= Bellone is also rumored to have directed a number hardcore X-rated features under the nom de porn "Torque Lambada", the most notorious picture being* FELT WOMAN; *a truly bizarre style clash*

*between stalk-n-slash menace, superhero adventure, rape revenge brutality, creature feature theatrics, and fuck film histrionics... performed by a cast of literal puppets and actors in puppet suits. when placed on a double bill with* STEAMED CANDY, *FELT* WOMAN *left golden age porn audiences and critics utterly bewildered, and the film went virtually unseen, though some of the puppeteers on the project did "graduate" to the local access children's variety program* SUCKER'S SOCIETY, *and the puppet of "Violata Rawends" is visible in the background of the doctor's office in* GASH LADDER.)

a work by N. Casio Poe

**THE FOLLOWING CRAWL HAS BEEN PAID FOR BY THE SECTARIAN KARNAGE AXIS:**

THE SECTARIAN KARNAGE AXIS EXTENDS ITS DEEPEST SUPPORT TO THE INDIVIDUAL YOU LEFT LEANING ME-DIARRHEA CLUBFOOTS HAVE DUBBED "SHY GUY", FOR COMMITTING THE HONOR KILLING OF THE FLESH-BETRAYER LAUGHABLY KNOWN AS "WOLF WARRIOR", WHO WORE OUR COLORS EITHER OUT OF PITIFUL OBLIVIOUSNESS OR A WEAK ATTEMPT AT NULLIFYING MOCKERY OF OUR UNSHAKABLE ETHOS.

THE VOIDED BOWELS OF THAT MAGGOT-RIDDEN SKIN-CRIME NOW PROVIDE SUCCOR FOR THE CERULEAN SWAN, WHOSE EMERGENCE WILL AFFIRM OUR VICTORY IN THE WHITE IRON BLOOD TSUMANI.

THE OVERWORKED TEAR DUCTS OF THOSE WHO TOSS THEIR SYMPATHY AWAY LIKE SO MUCH MULTI-CULTURAL GARBAGE ON DUPLICTIOUS LIBERAL RACE-TRAITORS AND MIGRATING VERMIN SKUNK-APES PRODUCE THE ICHOR THAT WILL RECIRCULATE THROUGH THE VEINS OF THE SLUMBERING BEHEMOTH YOUR SMOOTH TALKING COMMUNIST

{VOID}

SENSIBILITIES HAVE DENIED FOR FOR TOO LONG.

IT IS OUR DEMAND THAT THE SCUMBAITING GLOBALISTS CEASE ANY AND ALL PRODUCTION OF BORDER RAPING MUD LIVES MATTER "KILL KILL KILL THE WHITE MAN" PROPGAGHANDA, OR WE WILL HAVE NO RECOURSE BUT TO SMEAR THE WALLS OF YOUR LUXURY PEDO-DENS WITH THE MALODOROUS RECTAL TAR THAT OUR ENEMIES ERRONEOUSLY REFFER TO AS "SKIN".

MAY THE YOLK OF THEIR EXTREMITIES BE RENDERED THE TALLOW OF OUR CLEANSING.

**- "APEX ENABLER", RANCHOIR PRIEST OF S.K.A.**

*KIRITSIS' first willful sexual encounter was at age thirteen, when he was coaxed by his seventh grade art teacher LILIAN MEWLPYS... a softcore porn doppelganger of Mary Steenburgen... to stroke up and down her exposed cunt while feeding her slices of homemade sourdough rye bread that were shaped like ivory-poached elephant skulls. KIRITSIS hadn't thought about it for a long time, but the memory was jostled while watching the latest episode of SAVAGE BRUTALITY WRESTLING, when during his now weekly routine of deep-ogling heel manager*

*MS. MEGAN TIVITY ("a teenage dream if you hate yourself" according to color commentator Sweeny Potitus) he finally was able to pinpoint the resemblance she bears to the art teacher, the lure of his draw to her having dogged him for the past three weeks.*

spent the previous day catching up on the controversy surrounding Serenghetti Coup streaming Anna Kimikis' debut film *SWINEGRAVE;* a literally masturbatory coming-of-age arthouse autofiction about growing up in Jakarta during the 1990s, where she was became obsessed with film, music, and mythology while her parents made her work the summers in their butcher shop.

the controversy arose when the marketing department at Serenghetti created a poster that highlighted a scene where thirteen year old actress Alicia Sari is sitting in front of a mirror, legs spread, while she curiously considers inserting a severed pig hoof into her vagina, which going by the poster appears to be on route to lowering. a poor choice, but clearly one meant to ride on the outrage such an image might produce. the gambit backfired, and Serenghetti Coup lost a chunk of subscribers, as well as kicking up yet another emotional brushfire on the internet.

taken in context, the scene in question barely last 3 seconds, cutting away from the actress at the moment of the hog knuckle's breaching of the vaginal cavity...

{VOID}

a moment that is never shown, despite what the "testimonials" on sketchy alt-right and conspiracy theory platforms claim is present. Kimikis' intentions are too humorously poetic, if a bit morose, to be be considered exploitive, let alone pornographic. the scant handful of other scenes in the film relating to the character's budding sexuality are about equal in the prurient spectacle department to the benign instructional contents of a "your body and you" video, with a bit of the old subtext about the overwhelming power our genital's yield over all of us.

but this is America. we don't do subtext. we don't do nuance. least of all when it comes to examinations of sex. for U.S., sex is something to fear rather than anticipate, to laugh at rather than with , to be taken with force rather than shared with enthusiasm. and in the climate we unfortunately find ourselves occupying at the current stage in our collective development, anything that dares to veer away from those options is fodder for a singularly vicious but still depressingly typical puritanical pedo-panic cancel campaign, with some anti-intellectualism, surface level class warring, low-key xenophobia, and hostile misogyny thrown in for "good" measure.

i can't help but speculate on what exactly this kind of propulsive negative energy against "liberal Hollywood perverts" (film wasn't made in Hollywood, but ok) would accomplish were it directed toward ACTUAL child sex abuse and not controlled stagings of closed door adolescent touchstones that EVERY. SINGLE. ONE. OF. US. NO. FUCKING. EXCEPTION. has experienced. instead we get empty gestures that solve nothing and save no one.

the best this performative outrage displayed by the over-preoccupied social isolationists of the commentary space can hope to accomplish is ginning up a gaggle of culturally illiterate rubes to the point where they *gasp* *opt out of renewing their subscriptions* (OHHHH NOOOO) to the streaming video extension of a globalized corporate enterprise that itself is equipped with enough innumerable tentacle-spreads across a dizzying litany of media platforms that the mass exodus of a few moral-fetishists will inflict an impact on their place in the market comparable to the pinch of a single pubic lice on the lava-cauterized surface of a world-eating godbeast.

the worst outcome is more likely; that while the attentive concerns of those who are in a position to do some actual good.. protect some actual lives... are fixed and dilated toward the concave sensationalism of posting hot takes about misunderstood pop culture footnotes and the imagined ritual ugliness of socio-political opponents, the true ruin-ers of life will find this comically woeful diversion of time, finances, and resources ultimately advantageous, and continue their violations in banal plain sight.

{VOID}

that is the real exploitation; white nationalist splinter cells and fundamentalist religious groups recruiting members of polite society to their cause by claiming that they are "leading the fight" against child sex trafficking, "taking a stand against" the one thing we all can obviously agree is despicable and odious, when they have no real interest in going after those who actually abuse children (some of which are located in their own houses, congregating in the basement for a game of nephew torso ookie-cookie), just on smearing their perceived rivals in the false struggle between "good" (ie "us") and "bad" (ie "them").

tear lickers. cascading synesthesia. veins thinning from gale-force surges of carbonated battery acid. everyone should have been an only child.

drip of a sewer pipe looped through a network of synthesizers. trace the echo's reverb to a grated window outside my room. the drip fades into an electric piano riff, which when my crawl hits the surface explodes into snarling theatre punk, its decibels at war with the chainsaw propellers of a nearby helicopter, which maintains a satellite vigil over the crowd on Bannon Ave; costumed party goers gathered for the annual Nothtingun Sideshow Parade.

the highest concentration of street dwellers is in the junkyard directly across from the mirrored glass office building 5079 Bannon Ave, where a stage has been erected for a live band; a noisy industrial shoegaze act with deep soaring vocals that sounds like a cross between Plasmatics and Medicine.

due to a backdrop of large television screens the members of the band were obscured in blue-tinted shadow. the TVs were playing the "garrote spot" from SBW's first DNA Evidence match between Franco Sect and Florecido Condenar (on loan from the Mexico based CONTRA EL MUNDO LUCHA promotion) ... slowed to a crawl and color inverted, an homage to the blurred cable signals that those of us from a certain age remember attempting to thwart our budding dependence on hardcore pornography.

the frontperson of the group was the only one completely visible. despite the new slicked back silvery pink hair and large brown sunglasses, by the adorable gap in her front teeth, i recognize the vocalist as Natasha Stappo; a local author / cult survivor, who is wearing a green leather jacket over a shredded rubber body stocking that can't help but urge me to recall those old issues of *Wet Look* i was looking over a few days earlier.

as their set reaches its climax, Natasha convincingly feigns a series of violent convulsions, thrashing and shrieking like an immolated marmot sealed in burlap. the song ends, the whole band stares at the crowd from under their eyelids, and the screens go white. after roughly thirteen seconds, a face and a figure begin to emerge from the white. they appear to belong to a mermaid doll that had been submerged in a soap-clouded bathtub, bobbing back up to float in a view from the ceiling. its head is trunk of muddy clay, facial features established by the fingers of a child. across the chest of the doll there is a bra made of tiny bones, with two small skull heads as the cups. the tail of the doll is a swirl of arterial pinks and reds, the serrated paraffin scalloped to resemble the teeth of a sawblade.

"thanks everyone. we're THAT'S NOT GOOD I'M NOT HAPPY. fuck around and find out. k bye."

the lights on the stage go out. when they come back up, the band and the audience are gone. the stage sits collapse, waiting to assimilate into the detritus of the junkyard. the only evidence of a prior occupied capacity are steaming chunks of bomb-lobbed gore, roping the jagged shards of auto wreckage protruding from the makeshift shacks that have been erected by the hopelessly lost and the blissfully deranged.

there's a light weight on my left shoulder. a long tail coils up through my armpit to irritatingly tap at my cheek. there's a voice like frustrating anti-comedy in my ear.

"heyheyheyheyheyheyheyheyheyheyheyheyheyheyhe yheyheyheyheyheyheyheyhey"

"yeah Ratley hi. hi hi. we hear you. what is it?"

"juuuuuuuustoletyouknow.......LiafoundNogoz."

"OH FUCK WHAT THE FUCK THANK FUCK LET'S FUCK."

"......thatsmeanyouremeanandyoudon'tevenknow"

Ratley hops off my shoulder, running through the junkyard, growing bigger as he gets farther way. by the time he reaches Altomare Bridge, he's like a furry blue whale with limbs and diseases. as he sits up on his hind legs to tower over the bridge, another large creature emerges from the ocean on the opposite side. this beast... a bio-mechanical amalgam between a man and a wild pig... its head painted like a tattered American flag... is even larger than Ratley is now, so much so that Ratley once again finds himself to be the size he was while on my shoulder.

Ratley ducks under the bridge so he can climb up the greasy gearwork and steaming wet cables of the mechanized werepig. Ratley settles on a bulging chrome shoulder, and begins to chatter into the pig's ear, which causes its video game monster eyes to strobe. a cooking stove jawbone unhinges to spew a mushroom plume of gunmetal ash from behind its twisted metal tusks... color grading the sky with the crimsons and coppers of an out-of-control brushfire.

i come close to missing the renewed movements of the viscera strewing the grounds of the junkyard, evidently a response to the Indonesian haze overcasting the world. the guts and blood congregate into a bulk in front me, tangling themselves together into an enlarged cocoon. whomever is occupying the interior of the cocoon performs a series of push-ups, which eventually cause the cocoon to stand up right.

the cocoon begins to be raised by an unseen rope, dragged upward like the players of an elementary school production of *Peter Pan,* passing through an aquamarine cloud, where it disappears out of my sight.

*the in climate weather and the looming election cycles have been getting to KIRITSIS, so he found himself punching his stomach to relieve himself of the dog-piling tensions of the week, the singular after effects of that cathartic self-abuse being akin to the exaggerated remembrance of particularly heavy fetish sex sessions, where he found himself anxious to be destroyed for the sole purpose of breaking the caustic monotony of a beautiful woman.*

*KIRITSIS begs to be do(o)mmed.*

chilled piss. assault lament. vocation module. methane vigil. skeleton masks with vertical mouths. zippers of teeth that run from throat to brow. cleaver tools of the heavily bandaged. delinquent autocrat landscaping between a crematorium and a pornography store... pleated anus singing falsetto where the mollusk detached the rote accumulation of golem placenta shitting botched castrations on celibate microbes.

*the pessimistic malaise afflicting KIRITSIS was momentarily eschewed when he was able to locate a reasonably priced bootleg of* SPREADATORS; *a quite infamous Category III Hong Kong film.*

*written and directed by NORM YUNGAO,* SPREADATORS *recounts a "true life" crime story involving a husband and wife who work together to infect the population of their province with a dizzying array of diseases and illness. the wife (played with an alien sensuality by model/singer YAI PIM) works as a nurse at an infectious disease ward, where during her rounds she finds increasingly creative ways to collect blood, urine, stool, and (perhaps most notably) semen samples from the patients. the husband (a gonzo misanthropic performance from character actor WONG YAM) works as a chef at the popular Thirteen Angels Restaurant, where he expertly mixes the purloined DNA samples into the dishes he prepares and serves to the customers.*

*when doctors, customers, and police begin tracing their suspicions about the uptick in violent illness to the Thirteen Angels Restaurant, the husband and wife find themselves accelerating into a rampage period of increasingly gruesome murder, dismembering and burning anyone who crosses them. as their vicious mania increases, the "pigs from within need to be fed", and the husband and wife begin repurposing the human remains into morose sex toys for their perverted fetish games (the "burnt child train" set piece, where YAI and YAM perform something of a foursome with a pair of charred skeletons of a boy and girl they caught snooping around their dumpster, is frequently excised from most imported editions).*

*as the narrative propels into an localized apocalypse, the husband and wife find themselves on the receiving end of unbridled vigilante mob justice, being physically assaulted by the diseased residents of the province. the couple are eventually cornered in their apartment above the Thirteen Angels Restaurant, where they are bound together by rope, doused with lighter fluid, and set on fire.*

SPREADATORS *ends with the rope-bound corpses of the husband and wife fused together into a single mound of ash, upon which the residents of the province takes turn pissing... until all that's left of the couple is a foaming oil of watery black mud.*

LONG ISLAND VIDEO 13 NEWS REPORTING: after a bitterly contentious election cycle, the vote has been called for DENNY GATHERS, now President Elect of the United States, beating out incumbent DAX SPAMIN, who has been mounting an increasingly deranged offense against his opponent, going so far as to accuse GATHERS' party of either poisoning him or performing some kind of black magic cult ritual in order to "hijack the vote".

SPAMIN has been in a state of paranoid agitation since his collapse at a rally that was held at the Suasan Columns last summer, which aides attributed to "exhaustion". since then, SPAMIN's usual tirades have been laced with cryptic, almost occult-like references to "perverted monsters" who wish to "feast upon and gang rape" his corpse.

after the final results were tallied, SPAMIN used his concession speech to say the following;

"i did not lose... i just got tired of winning. i know the chalk hearts of the demoncracks. in many ways i am still trapped within their maze of knotted tunnels... which are full of teeth that grind within the neon slime of a tablespoon cataract. i did not lose, but i am lost."

it was later revealed that much of

this speech was a series of mangled quotations from the racist novel CERULEAN SWAN, published by the violent neo-Nazi splinter group SECTARIAN KARNAGE AXIS (SKA), which has been designated a terrorist cell, ironically by the SPAMIN administration.

after roughly thirteen more minutes of what even his staunchest supporters described as needlessly morose navel-gazing self-pity, SPAMIN then walked away from the podium, "Free to Decide" by The Cranberries playing him out over the sound system.

shortly after SPAMIN's speech, Vice President Elect SALOME THRILWELL was heard to remark;

"well, he really put the 'bent' in 'incumbent', eh?"

the SPAMIN campaign could not be reached for further comment, though there have been rumors of Spamin planning to launch his own media conglomerate tentatively known as SPAMIN ACTION KINGDOM (SAK), with intentions to challenge business rival CHANCE CAVE's company SERENGHETTI by having its own web shop and streaming platform with original programming.

more as this story develops.

fuck out my eyes with kitchen forks. visuals and narrative perpetually whipsaw between deconstruction and reconstruction with the unpredictable pacing of a child's dark imagination... exposing the caustic indifference and punishing judgments of friends and family when your desperate struggles form a blockade around the lifeforce they need to drain from you to sustain their own positions of ascent. every toiletry dunce cap who thinks the coming-of-age redundancy of a glorified Tik-Tok video is the pinnacle of brutality one can inflict upon a child should be forced to watch a near thirteen hour trauma loop of numbing human degradation until the surfaces of the billiard balls occupying their cranial interiors peel into rinds of oozing blisters.

How 'bout they can both be president as long as they share one giant suit at all times?

sorry... i misspelled "noose".

fat jackal bone occupation. petrified crucifix. fissures wink 'neath tender masks. backwash tents their cheekbone sponge. persistent revenge. fabric scalpels.

**{VOID}**

stigmata lapels. leashed seeds cutting wrath. interchangeable grifters hasten a blueprint of imagined maleficence. somehow both skittish china dolls and violent masterminds of intricate crimes trees. daylight savings body clock illuminating rape-stage. ruin slicked with barren shrieks snapped pink their dulcet cream. cracked-line hammertoes scratch out the phantom mites at the false anal void.

she is held upright with a thin white cord that has been looped around her neck, the slack tied to a steel hook just where the wall meets the ceiling. her arms are tied together behind her back, forcing the stomach and chest forward, making her torso appear to be limbless. her legs are spread fairly wide, the feet locked inside wire-frame booties that have been bolted to cinderblocks.

long rubber hoses have been inserted into her vaginal and anal cavities. the clear tubes are each attached to equestrian syringes, their barrels full of a rust-colored liquid matter. the syringes are soon picked up by clawed hands, gloved in a dark blue latex. the index and middle fingers slide into the circular grips atop the flanges of the plungers, becoming cereal box decoder rings below the knuckles of the claws. the plungers are pressed down, user-ing the surge of the rotted metal cocktail into the entry and exit points for his bodily wants.

dimpled face tenses, white rows of the mouth gritting

against their edges in the presentation of the maw. the fluid of the syringes swells her organs until her abdominal protrusion looks to be in the not-too-late-but-not-too-early stage of pregnancy, when the testicular larva starts to resemble a gummy-bear fruit snack version of a curled up infant.

once the last of the fluids has voided the barrels of the syringes, the rubber hoses are removed from the cavities by the clawed latex hands. the wielder of those pointed mitts steps into view; a zipper-mouthed bipedal machine... a steroidal sewing box doll stitched together an animated by a child molesting seamstress witch. he scans and grazes the squirming woman, whose core strength threatens to max out from the pinched-nerve stress of simultaneous bladder and bowels voiding being indefinitely withheld.

the burly apparition settles to the slight of her lefthand side. a tightly balled fist lands just above her navel with the hiccupping thud of a slaughterhouse cattle husk being softened under the impact of a spiked mallet. more blows follow, hitting the center and side of her solution-bloated gut, until the contents of the syringes drop out from her ass and cunt... burgundy splash back coating her lower extremities in a miscarriage-dye.

cycling back to the rape fantasy netherworld of DAXIS's *BLUE GLOOM* series. haven't been able to find more information on this "Mona Grub" actress.

her age could be anywhere from late 20s to early 50s, but she could also be showing the wear-and-tear of an overlived teenager. research about Thylacine (aka "SadisValiK") led me down a rabbit hole that included moody upper-tier gay pornography and an RLSV ( "real-life supervillain") operating under the name "Thylacine", who was a friend-enemy (probably much more, given his likes-to-fuck vocation) of the deceased RLSH known as Rawdog.

*KIRITSIS finds his thoughts returning to the THAT'S NOT GOOD I'M NOT HAPPY show from a night or two earlier, specifically the video that played on the background screens. a side effect of viewing this clip was the recovery of a deeply submerged recollection with regards to an event from KIRITSIS' childhood.*

*while being left in the care of family friends, KIRITSIS was left to explore their home; an abandoned administrative building that had been converted into a squat by and for what KIRITSIS would much later come to understand as a rather loose knit cult called THE REFUSGE... so much in the most free of free forms that their malaise restricted them from even having a central leadership, only a vague reference to a quartet of unseen sisters.*

*eventually, KIRITSIS found a part of the building that looked like a grade school auditorium, sneaking to the upper-most left corner of the seating rows. red velvet curtains were drawn closed on the stage, pocked with a jaundice fungi that resembled foaming tufts of yeast. from just above KIRITSIS's right ear, a stage direction is barked;*

*"JERK CURTAIN"*

*the crushed sheet of bulbing mold separates, allowing for a beam of floodlight to illuminate the stage. a topless woman was sitting on a large wooden crate, wearing a long tight skirt that forced her to position her legs as if they were the tail of a mermaid. nursing at her left breast was a baby that looked to be armored in scabs both fresh and flaking, its inverted lips clacking in futile orbit over the pristine nipple like an inside-out armadillo.*

*with her available arm, the woman reached behind the crate, producing a tall box. the box was connected to the crate by a tangled bulk of cords. at the top of the box there was a lever, its rubbery grip positioned opposite the woman and baby. the woman reached for the lever, locking her fingers tight around the grip, and pulled it toward her, until it lay aiming at her side.*

*with one last downward nudge, the lever clicked at the top of the long box, which was followed soon by the sudden eruption of crate, showering the stage with smoke and splinters, sending the woman and the baby in all directions at once, the walls and floor of the stage smeared in brownish purple spray patterns.*

**{VOID}**

*"CARLTON!"*

*the name is called out with all the incredulity of a sitcom big sister. KIRITSIS scurried out of the auditorium, finding a spot where he could pretend to read the latest issue of REVULSIONARY VIDEO magazine, hoping his babysitter would be none the wiser.*

*further remembrances of the immediate surrounding of that day became glitchy for KIRITSIS. many years later, while deep into the study of the world's prehistory at THE FRACTURE COMPOUND, a speculative factoid seemed to infer that REVULTICKS were in fact the resultant spawn of mating acts between SKAVILKADVRIS and PIENTAVIDDAN: a seldom-referenced oceanic Gargantua that the more arcane-focused annotators of folk tales and mythology have considered to be the knotted root at the basis of all mermaid lore.*

*none of these lore-spelunking monks have gone so far as to literarily ruminate on a physical description of PIENTAVIDDAN, nor have any sketch artists or sculptors ventured to do the same.*

*in a since deleted online review of NATASHA STAPPO's cult-survivalist memoir SCARECROW REVOLT, which those who are easily overwhelmed by superstition have opted to paint as a modern era grimoire, the anonymous critic invoked both the names of SKAVILKADVRIS and PIENTAVIDDAN, singling them out as the likely parentage of THE CRAWLION and THE BEAUTANT; vividly described in STAPPO's book as hormone-devoted creatures that emerge to indulge their appetites during periods of extreme repression (anger in the case of CRAWLION, sexual in case of THE BEAUTANT), causing violent emotional overrides of the carefully maintained social composures stagnating those times.*

*the comment thread on this post grew sizable, with the anonymous critic assuredly laying out his theory that THE CRAWLION was born of a GORGRE matron after having fucked SKAVILKADVRIS, and THE BEUTANT was born of PIENTAVIDDAN after being gang-raped by a pack of NOSANGUINES.*

*the final comment before the entire thread was torched was believed to have been a meticulously detailed deep-dive exposition of the CYSYTISSM society's most infamous ritual; the summoning of either THE CRAWLION or THE BEAUTANT for purposes of heightening their already elaborately violent sex games (either party goers or the beings becoming pregnant seemed incidental, which is in keeping with the curious indifference often displayed by the society).*

indifferent curiosity. experience reduced to story reduced to think piece reduced to sound bite reduced to click bait reduced to hot take. exiled from the decadent misanthrope cool dude club because they discovered my pornographic tastes and turn-ons tended to veer toward performers, creators, positions, scenarios, imagery, and reactions i find attractive and/or interesting, instead of feigning a pretense toward achieving placement within the upper most tier of gritty artful perversion because they profess to only obtain arousal while watching the casually passionless degradation of a skeletal junkie whose visible abuse causes them to resemble a decaying 1970s felt ventriloquist dummy that had been left to soak in a rain logged dumpster.

dispute events. necro botanical plaque gauze. backlash shit-sauce recruitment pool. virgin sensitivities have regenerated to almost total in the hiatal twilight of this over logged exile. weaponized neural apathy pressurizing torrid inclinations. lacerate deliberation beading edge of teeth. muscle curls a gutter cone where the rupture can slide. vascular brushstrokes upholster the lung brings. ultraviolet vegetation scaling ganglia walls. the trash your garbage throws away. the peanut butter smell of dried rubber gloves. superpowered burn victims get theirs in the third act. deflective mirth rooting the core of a closet pig. i know you from my search history.

... exhausted from feigning ironic detachment... from internalizing torrid inclinations until viscera becomes mulched in the corrosive enzymes repression has made of all the dammed DNA evidence.... these fetishes do indeed comment on the wider power structures undergirding our existence... but they also speak to deeper fascinations that when pulled from under the skin and exposed to restless light consume the neural networks with a beautifying purity that even the most fully realized of pornographic recreation can only condescend to whisper of its overwhelming satisfaction...

*KIRITSIS discovers a promotional one-sheet for a dwarfsploitation film out of Russia called* THE SADEAN HOMUNCULUS. *physical evidence of what was initially believed to only have existed within the fuzzily insisted recall of a Deja-vu occurrence.*

THE SADEAN HOMUNCULUS *starred SERGEI PRIAVAWN (who also served as writer and director) as "Kart"; a diminutive peeping tom who lives within the walls of a "last stop" youth hostel that he inherited from his absentee mother, spying on the transients and the staff of the building. Kart's voyeurism begins to expand into pranks and manipulations, all for what at first is benign amusement, but eventually graduates into a grim spitefulness that dovetails into callow prurience as he begins to sexually violate and brutally murder the transients, dismembering them so he can create a cadaverous sex doll out of the parts he likes best, which he will use until it is, as he puts it, "a mulch of rot prints on my cock!", a refrain Kart sings over the end credits.*

*PRIAVAWN would reprise this role, this time giving the character a full name and new job, when he played "Warden Kart Vilkurik" in GENE MURIFALT's scorched earth women-in-prison epic* SHACKLE LABYRINTH, *which featured an all-star who's who of exploitation sirens as the prison population (YOLANDA KLATE, RHEA UHUA, RACINA MOLIV, MONICA DUPONT, and fresh-faced newcomer YAI PIM), with adult film star DELIAH VALISE as their dangerously voracious cell block unit manager "Pia Detriesse", who orchestrates their many degradations with the full support and backing of the staff, the officers, and of course Warden Kart Vilkurik.*

*soon after* SHACKLE LABYRINTH, *PRIAVAWN would go on to once again write and direct and act, crafting what he thought would most appeal to a slightly more broad swath of the American movie market. the result was* STRUNG UP WITH CARE; *a Christmas-themed surrealist anti-comedy splatter film. PRIAVAWN played a supporting role this time; the disgruntled elf accomplice to a mass murdering mall Santa played by BRADLEY GUNNAR, a few years before he would take on the role of "Greasetrap" in the* SOW *franchise (it's widely believed that VINCENZO SCAPPELI was inspired by* STRUNG UP WITH CARE *to cast GUNNAR in the lead role for* SOW; *his own much more conventional, and therefore successful, stab at the cinematic wet market that was the 1980s slasher craze).*

*looking and playing like a John Hughes movie from a child murdering hell dimension whose citizenry is held under the despotic control of an art-damaged pervert sect,* STRUNG UP WITH CARE *failed to catch on in the States, frustrating PRIAVAWN enough to take an extended hiatus from the business.*

*roughly thirteen years after the disappointment of* STRUNG UP WITH CARE, *PRIAVAWN would reemerge, and so would his "Kart" character, in a truly strange trio of* SADEAN HOMUNCULUS *sequels, produced for the made-on-demand mail order video company C.R.E.S.T. PRODUCTIONS, known best for producing brutally unusual fetish vignettes at the request of their viewers, which were only available through the C.R.E.S.T. catalog. the sequels would reach a mass audience years later as bonus features on* DEGRANULATE's *expanded edition Blu-Ray/DVD combo of* THE SADEAN HOMUNCULUS. *this releases would renew interest in* STRUNG UP WITH CARE., *which would finally find its place among the syllabus of Happy Holiday Horror. a special edition release is reportedly in the works, once again from DEGRANULATE.*

mung helmet. a cracker box pours out cicada shells into the forceps' gap. spit-roasted on glass dildos they have filled with bees. well shit, if my first two years on this malignant sewage orb were 2019 and 2020, I'd be taking my cues from Connor Clapton as well. i just want a clit that can fuck me.

*it's a slow late weeknight at SEDGEWICK'S GRIND HOUSE, the local coffee bar / performance venue, which KIRITSIS tends to prefer, as he can slip into a cushioned booth and indulge the jitters while decluttering the hoard in his head.*

*the evening's peace of porcelain clacking ambient tones and low-volume early '00s rock hits is abruptly abated when a pair of roadkill valentines kick open the door hard enough for the playlist to hiccup during Abandoned Pools "The Remedy". his arms are wrapped around her shoulders and hers around his waist, clad in matching gummed leather jackets and denim pants the weeks have worn down to browning green skin flaps, not so much cackling as they are gargling excess lung fluid in obnoxious bliss, their aesthetic screaming "just a Joker looking for his Harley".*

*KIRITSIS recognizes the pair; EZRA KRUGE and IDA CARUTHERS-KRUGE. KIRITSIS remembers IDA from school; three grades beneath him... always around those three grades above her (and sometimes four or five... EZRA being a five). she looks to have put on about thirteen pounds of muscle in her arms and thighs, but maintains the build in such a way that she looks soft and round upon first sight... though her stance does undermine any intentions of looking like a push over.*

*as for EZRA, KIRITSIS only knows him through*

*observation. two grades above him in school, he always struck KIRITSIS as a poser and a braggart, really buying into the notion of his slightly above average looks being his ticket to fame and fortune. he looks more gaunt now... eyes sunken deep to the back of his skull from the exhaustion of trying to look as good as he did when he peaked, long hair still full and think, but heavily sprayed to look wet all the time.*

*last KIRITSIS heard, EZRA and IDA moved to Methuke, a particularly odious suburb of Florida (if one can imagine), after EZRA's brother ELMER had something like a nervous breakdown when he discovered that his love object IDA had been fucking his older brother, which led to him losing his job and having a brief stay at IRIS THACHER MEMORIAL ASYLUM (while it was still operating in a more "official" capacity).*

*it's somewhere in the space between "Smile Like You Mean It" by The Killers bleeding into "Bandages" by Hot Hot Heat that IDA cocks her head upon the sight of KIRITSIS, who guns down the last gulp of his 48 hour blend. IDA nudges at EZRA's ear to get his attention, followed by a motion toward KIRITSIS. one tacit nod later, the willfully conjoined pair of natural born doom generators slide into KIRTSIS' booth.*

*"hey... sorry to bother you... but did you go to Hawntag High School?"*

*"occasionally."*

**{VOID}**

*"yeah yeah yeah.... Carlton, right?"*

*"yuh. hi, Ida."*

*"oh shit you remember me huh? i was so nervous around you all the time, y'know?"*

*KIRITSIS is sure that she's thinking of someone else, as he has no recollection of a young IDA ever being in his orbit... but those days are a blur.*

*KIRITSIS perks up when he hears the opening strains of She Wants Revenge's "Take the World", leaving EZRA and IDA to linger in awkward silence, which EZRA volunteers to break.*

*"listen brother, we've been on the road for almost as long as that coffee of yours has been on the burner. it's our honeymoon, y'know? y'hear this song going right now? well yeah... i'd like to get to some of that before i collapse, aight?"*

*(the song going on is "Fuck the Pain Away" by Peaches)*

*"so hell yeah brother, got any motel recommendations?"*

*"ehhh... well i was recently at the Sky Inside Motel in Shareboy. it's about 30 minutes from here."*

*"nothing closer?"*

*"nothing worth recommending."*

**{VOID}**

*nearing the end of "Honest Mistake" by The Bravery, EZRA and IDA exit the booth, with IDA shooting what KIRITSIS is sure he is erroneously reading as a 'i'd hit that" look. his eyes take in one last drink of her backside, which has the dubious honor of becoming an image that will be triggered every time KIRITSIS hears Phantom Planet's "California".*

*there was once a time where KIRITSIS wanted what EZRA and IDA have; a consenting dual partnership in socially maligned proclivities. believing he had found such an accomplice in PIXY DEVILLE, he momentarily broke his walls down, pulling back the layers so the turned worms of his underside could for a first time rut in the daylight. PIXY's recoil and revulsion when encountering these visions of suffering left KIRITSIS marked with the conclusion that his deepening need to actualize his internalized criminality was perhaps best indulged alone... that the way it was meant to be shared was as a captured image a postcard rendered glossy, with a return address from a solitary confinement holding cell in the root-bowels of a black site medical facility.*

*not that KIRITSIS has ever found a time for this track or band that was ever really appropriate or necessary, but in light of the previous moment of clarity, "The Middle" by Jimmy Eat World can't help itself but feel like it's taking on a tone of acute mockery.*

**{VOID}**

# BLUE YOLK

LONG ISLAND VIDEO 13 NEWS REPORTING: the Sky Inside Motel once again became the scene of violence, as police engaged in a shootout with EZRA KRUGE and IDA CARUTHERS-KRUGE; the infamous "Roadkill Valentines", who have been cutting a swath of murder and mayhem up the east coast for the past 13 days, starting in Methuke, Florida with the revenge-motivated home invasion of a recently released convict acquaintance of the pair.

according to detectives NORGLAM and OPASTOP, THE KRUGES had evidently taken a family hostage at the hotel, breaking into their room in the middle of the night. the husband, wife, and two children were indeed among the victims of the shootout, but it remains unclear whether they were killed deliberately by the KRUGES or accidently by police.

after a theatrical display of surrender, both EZRA KRUGE and IDA CARUTHERS-KRUGE were placed under arrest. they are currently awaiting trial, which is already all but guaranteed to be a sensationalistic affair, as the duo has already developed something of a folk-cult following.

when asked to comment on the couple's popularity, Detective Norglam responded;

"i've literally seen and heard everything. nothing surprises me anymore. there are certainley no shortage of sick, sad, weird people out there who for some reason choose to worship freakishly evil specimens like THE KRUGES, but i try not to concern myself with them... until they take it too far."

we'll have more as this story develops.

the dreaming leech a script attendant. fibrous bio-chassis pulped to grains on a hatchet the blows have polished to glass. an eight-foot man stoops forward and contorts his upper body until he appears to be half his own height, racked with an overwrought survivor remorse that remains permanently locked on the edge a cancer scare invokes, transcribing doomed romance and other redundancies in a mail bomber shack of fluorescent light tubes. take this chicken with a fist and mumble raw slurs with the rhythm of a chant until made lesser than its knuckle-fucked gum-wad. print out the death threats to your children and send them to me because i need something real to masturbate to.

*"fuck my mouth until the floor is a mirror i can drown in"* - from "Cum Dumpster Fire." by SYREN VEDA K, off the album *Turtle Vision.*

filter shroud. wet gait comes epileptic as a reeling teaser, fingers pruned from disinfectant. velveteen mound of noble rot settles the agreed upon targets of mayonnaise-spiced holocaust advocates. a gridded dome of broken teeth that inhaling celestial gore has ballooned into a chromium neon eyeball, tentacle-slides in ruined spirals like the lolling thrash of degenerate tongues.

foreskin combover. cut off from the manic-juiced plasma i need in order to function while the childish imbeciles who engineered my exile remain privy to the access point of its telltale calcification. Ebola lepers strode raw bulbs of pipe, huffing the liquid essence of mid-shitting dust mites, parched gullets occupied by rain-swollen mushrooms latticed with scabs.

*the recent half-week found KIRITSIS on an internalized sabbatical from the multiverse within, as he attempted to wrangle his scattered energies and funnel them into one sole operation of focus; namely*

CHROME STALKS, *his long-running but sporadically released outlaw mini-comic that he writes and draws under the pen-name "SNOREN BOREGANS" and releases under the company name "MEGAN'S LOL".*

CHROME STALKS *tells the story of VIVAISKA; a mute barbarian "clothed in her own scar tissue" on route to a music and arts festival called CHROME STALKS, where attractions include intergender death match wrestling, stand-up anti-comedy, transgressive literature readings, and aberrant sex shows, all under "the blood-hazed skies of a mutilated universe". when she reaches the festival, VIVAISKA intends to kill MOUE; the festival's shady sponsor and leader of the cultish crime syndicate that trafficked her when she was a child. VIVAISKA managed to escape, scraping by at night in the desperate AMPUPLANTATIONS after training in the day in the PETRIFIED THICKET; a network of sewer tunnels that had become overwhelmed with sharp branches and thorn bushes.*

*each issue swaps between VIVAISKA's wordlessly hardscrabble journey through the excoriatingly crowded vastness of the AMPUPLANTATIONS and MOUE at CHROME STALKS itself, marinating in his repugnant decadence until all the prose is noble rot purple. MOUE's headquarters is the abandoned DANCING STAR COMPLEX shopping mall, the CHROME STALKS festival being held in the parking lot. MOUE is defined by a thinning mane of hay-textured white guy dreads, a sleep apnea mask molded to look like the licking mouth of a sexy lady, and a stretched out 4XL t-shirt with a picture of a mutilated infant whose limbs and joints are connected to each other by melting logs of shit. MOUE is usually surrounded by his "lieutenant" RIZ DASPAJUN; an elfin child predator who wears baby doll dresses and ultra-wide straight legged jeans, and RACK MELISMA; MOUE's "laconically lysergic" in-house composer, who is like what would happen if The Great Kat and the Doof Warrior had a baby and that baby grew up to be a metalcore version of Tonetta.*

*KIRITSIS initially concieved of* CHROME STALKS *while he was playing in SWORN VIRGIN. initially he had hoped for issues of the mini-comic to be packaged with SWORN VIRGIN releases, as a nod to his favorite toy line* HOMUNCULORDS. *SWORN VIRGIN only lasted long enough for a split release, so the idea never came to fruition, but KIRITSIS decided to forge ahead with* CHROME STALKS *anyway, making each issue only slightly bigger than a religous tract one might stumble upon while inspecting the curbside of the walk they're traversing. KIRITSIS even went so far as to make that his inital distribution model; leaving issues in the grass on the sidewalk across from LIMER'S POND.*

*it's not an irregular occurence for issues of*

CHROME STALKS *to be released years apart from each other, and for the issues themselves to waver in devotion to the overriding narrative, becoming vessels for whatever random floaters have been grazing the creative engines of KIRITSIS, be they a bout of bleary-eyed nostalgia or a debilitating ramble of pornographic frustration.*

*nevertheless, KIRITSIS maintains the word he made to himself to keep chipping away at the world of* CHROME STALKS... *that it will end when it wants to end, its conclusion removed from the will of KIRITSIS.*

heroin scarecrow. navel gouda. the shitting half of a split cow washed up in sea foam so thick that a dog was lost. inadvertent catalyst violated expectations with logic-derailing mantras until they were as common and thin as a whirring fleet of clumsy suburban drones.

functioning micro-television screens cover the total surface of a floating mannequin, each projecting its own live-feed from an alternate universe, flicking of their own volition through multiple timelines. though still irrational and alien, the jarring transition to corporeal actualization has reduced these mythos to a disturbing flatness, as if they had been injected with an anti-venom cocktail of broad swath banality... depleting their ichor of any and all inspiri-ative properties.

the screens begin to coordinate their imagery into a singular vision that washes over the scope of the featureless womanly shape; an infinite made material by guts and gore... the blood and offal imitating the structure of a galaxy. these arterial red cosmos begin to shift in color, the reclamation of that splatter-crimson shade seizing to the exponential struggle as the muted comforts of bleak greys and cold blues feel more conducive to the settling death of the universal gulf.

from the centered distance, a larval egg expands like a plume across the sternum of the floating mannequin, gradually molding its ancient wet grist into a totem of drowned burnt harridans ....

*The pendulum of the grandfather clock rocks like a metronome that keeps in perfect time with the harsh violins inside KIRITSIS' head, creating a metallic symphony suitable for yard sale sycophants and their plastic-clutching void-bound seedlings. he remembers the time PIXY DEVILLE did an elevated karaoke rendition of 50 Foot Hose's version of "God Bless the Child". she wore a dark silver latex gown with a bandoleer of kitchen knives across the chest, a mesh veil hanging from under the brim of a purple fedora like mosquito netting, and a black felt arm band with bloody super-hero emblem embroidered in the middle. the cord of a ribbon microphone being fondled by her carefully manicured fingernails... nail polish the color of curated dinosaur remains. her hair floats in mid-air in a fashion not dissimilar to the way it looks beneath the water when she lets her head wade and bob almost of its own will, paint chips flaking off the ceiling and hitting the water like the feathers of tiny birds.*

*KIRITSIS stops to stare at his reflection in the mirror. The sink is below the mirror. he pulls out his penis and begins to urinate into the sink. he looks down, amazed at the length of his pissing. It seems to get thicker and darker, becoming a whirlpool that seems to wash over the entire surface of the sink. The torrent of urine slows to a viscous crawl, becoming a thick paste smudging the porcelain. he looks back up at the mirror, and the face staring back at him is covered in the bluish urine paste, pushing even thicker, darker paste between the cracks of its teeth. The reflection then takes a gob of the paste in its hands. It opens its mouth and spreads it across the teeth and tongue, gagging and laughing. He looks down and finds that the sink is over flowing with the piss clay, and that he himself is covered in it. lifts his hands to the sides of his head, massaging the clay into his head, as if it were a leave-in conditioner. he then inspects his hands, which are pawing this paste/clay, and proceeds to smear it over the mirror, blocking out his demonic reflection.*

It's like they don't know what's happening, But they understand why it's happening. It's giving all their frustration a voice, A sound, something they can describe, And the frustration is doing the same to the sound; giving it a purpose, Making something alien something Tangible... constrictive to constructive. We indulge our absolutes. You are merely their keepers. The volume of our person will cause our inflamed bodies to emit greasy columns of smoke that roll over the vista, caking the land in thick grey primer, which when dried we will repaint nature without own flesh and blood. Reality is merely an epidermis. It can be peeled off the bones of the earth to reveal the viscera truth. " acts of god" or "miracles" are reality self-immolating. This is known among us...the light-flesh. And we are reaching out to you from alkaline nightmare, where we are at all time...yours and ours. spackling the walls with gummed up cerebral works. muscles and bones would erupt out of flesh, skinless form scaling the walls, leaving a trail of offal pearls in its wake. the charnel monster would than pull the meat from gory frame, running it over impossibly bronzed body, painting cooing face and twitching erogenous zones with arterial lacquer, gestures becoming more animalistic and primal as they orgasm, falling into a cannibal satisfaction on the mangled bedsheets that they have made of skin, enveloped in organ for all time. I can see it now...carried on the shoulders of those released of guilt . Those whose mind's eyes have been forever relieved of liberal society's cultural stigmatism implants. Those who have ripped that limp wristed suicidal insanity from themselves and adhered it to a once anemic reality that insists the myopic tunnel mud upon itself.

- from *Cerulean Swan* by SKA (Apocatheid Books)

hydrangea showerheads. Papers float like bleached lily pads. orange clouds trimmed with dusk-brushstrokes of purple. yellow flames wrap from their underside. brown cricket on blue floor ripped in half by a set of child hands. upper half tossed aside, the lower half still clutched. A bottle of dish-cleaning liquid. lid flipped off, dropping down like a severed head. pours the liquid on the wound of the split insect. red and white fizzing coming out of the abdomen like beer head. squeezes tightly on the abdomen, choking it until a wheezing scream emits from the exo-carcass.

astral molestation response unit. a stable of swelling heads filter a trough of bacteria. Exotic dancers with massive head wounds leaking like gynecological punctures. Auto-erotic immolation Like raping your twin sister; Only she will ever understand.

..i loathe appetite. the satisfaction after it is quelled is nothing  but gas, interfering with the expression it was supposed to have  made possible. I  hope  for  sick  oranges,  for cloud_cover on fire, for a bee_hive holocaust that incites riots between the multitude of insect kingdoms...

- from *Laconique* by Simone Vanique (translated from French by Ghislaine Nudesco for Villation Books)

the surface of the pool is covered with assorted dead insects; beetles, flies, wasps, and cicadas. when a half decomposed corpse bobs up from the water. The jaw of the skull flops open, scant flies emerging, chased by a spider that comes out of the skull like a black deformed tongue. The remaining skin around the skull is a cold green mold on the bone. the spider living in the jaw  guida the movements of the head. a wall of security televisions bursts up from the water. Some are broken, screens completely gone, wires hanging from where the glass used to be, like gutted animals whose intestines hang from rotting abdominal wounds. The images on the working TVs are so grainy that they are impossible to make out even at close range. when getting a closer look, the images grow even more distorted and hallucinogenic, further punctuated by the loud static that distorts the sounds into audio akin to rabbits being boiled in cooking oil. Gobs of saliva run down the televisions and start to boil into froth as the sounds get louder and louder, the spit-rivulets smoking when they hit the surface of the pool.

*metallic buzz echoing off the walls like a jostled hornet nest. KIRITSIS' bed is covered in bloody feathers. A full-grown body writes under the sheet. Stains begin spreading under the sheet at the knees, chest, and face of the body beneath. A window by the bed is sunburned with filth. A woman's hand presses against the glass, then runs across the surface, smudging it with dirt streaks.*

*a voice like a locust sinking in an upturned pencil sharpener drags the auditory equivalent of piano wire through KIRITSIS' ear canal.*

*"i'm HADASSAH."*

*with the extended enunciation of the last two letters of her name still vibrating his molecules, the underside tulpa HADASSAH SIVICK has appeared before him; hair and eyes the color of television static, tongue clacking pigskin teeth from a snarling chalk mouth.*

*HADASSAH's hand goes toward the stained bed, clutching at the sheet and pulling it off the bed. The hand spins the sheet like a bull-fighter's cape, twirling it to the floor. The stains spiral down the white, turning it into a barber shop cone. The body under the sheet is male, coated in mud-thick blue ink,*

{VOID}

*his features heavily caked in cerulean filth.*

*"have you met my son SEAMUS?"*

*SEAMUS is shivering and twitching, screaming loudly and covering his ears as the metallic buzzing becomes unbearable to contain.*

Chlorine greens and nighttime purples color a room filled with dust-caked iron lungs. Giant white cobwebs connect them together, as if wolf spiders had inherited the den. A big grey door with a small window in the shape of a cat's eye opens. Slow moving, sulphuric yellow smoke moves through the hallway. An exotic, shapely black haired woman steps out of the smoke and into full view. She walks between the lungs, clad in a red silk robe trimmed with thin gold dragons, toward a one-person shower. The ceiling is one big tile of florescent light, making the room look like the inside of a refrigerator. The showerhead is large and shaped like a pyramid with tiny bullet wounds. She takes off her robe, dropping it behind her, than kicking it out into the iron lung mortuary. She starts the shower. Water comes out of the bullet wounds, looking harsh and black, like scratches on a film reel. her backside is covered with continent size wounds, as if impetigo scabs had been peeled off prematurely. the largest, most severe wounds being across her ass, specifically the left cheek. There are light brown window blinds buried in the viscera. beads of water gather at the border of her wounds, but never enter.

Don't think we don't know. We know you know. You only go out For you. But only until there is only a convenience in your solutions. Until your dog's dream themselves out of your reality and all that can be ascertained from their telling is that once upon a time a word could Be in the same sentence twice, and then the following thought could take what was thought before and double it and theoretically every Line would birth sets of twins that eventually would be different enough that some could confuse that with genuine breeding when really it's just thinly veiled multiplicity. But then again, endless rats are inherent when you examine the actuality of thoughts not being infinite... in fact they are rarely such. More often then not, they are merely mutated and bastardized from something someone heard or read, and the interpretations are so lost beyond the pale that they become new ideas, when really they are just mistakes with a race tag that won't anchor them to the definition of what they really are.

- from *Cerulean Swan* by SKA (Apocatheid Books)

*photogenic daylight. Clouds are thin and flat on the sky. The ground is littered with toys, most of them broken. Doll arms and legs between blades of grass, as if someone planted seeds for a tree of limbs. a doll torso, which is pale cream colored with little muddy scratches about the neck, arm sockets, and leg sockets. It is resting against a thick wooden pike, grass growing around it as if it emitted a fertilizer through its atoms. tiny hand wraps around the doll torso, picking it up. LAYLA is wearing horn rimmed glasses, inspects the torso, standing next to an apple-green mail box. black hair fashioned into one long braid that she has swung over her left shoulder.*

*the street seems to go on forever. The is a black shape in the distance, moving like a ink scribble that grows the more your hands move. LAYLA takes notice of KIRITSIS at the other end of the street. She moves to the road to get at eye level with the strange thing... its movements akin to a silent movie frame. KIRITSIS gets closer and closer to the cautious but precocious little girl.*

*The two stare at one another, as if their routines had been interrupted, as if they both did the same thing every day, but only now they notice the other existed. What at first looks to be a long, black finger begins trailing LAYLA's left cheek, stating at the corner of her mouth. It leaves a thick, runny streak from the corner of her lips to her ear lobe. LAYLA gets smaller and smaller as KIRITSIS slowly ascends into the sky... becoming flat, black cloud that has taken its place among the fluffier white opposites.*

*LAYLA is looking up. Blood is running down the left side of her face. Half of the skin of her cheek hangs in a flap, revealing her jaw like a dental x-ray made flesh. She acts as if someone had drawn a silly picture on the side of her face, and goes back to the lawn, collecting the limbs her fits had sewn into the earth.*

finger them into submission... braid my cavities with their veins. walking behind Limer's pond. i spot a decaying Nosanguine, who is in a wheel chair, his bones twisted. he is moaning "LIIIIV" out of his crooked, drooling mouth. the Nosanguine resembled a grandfather that has been dead for thirteen years who was injected in the heart with some radioactive sludge to bring him back to life. He gradually becomes more human, but he is still childlike, as the years of being dead have left his brain little more than pinkish grey jelly sloshing around inside his skull. the Nosanguine looks up at the sky and bears his teeth, which are covered in cheap black wax, the sky behind him erupting in a constellation of cigarette burns.

swaying beneath the legion-crunch of scuttling roaches, women in surgical bondage gear performing mock surgery on pig intestines. A baby found sleeping in the street lane was sexually abused, than throttled to death by vinyl gloved hands. Crescentic orifices were modeled with fingernails on the soft pink flesh, than violated repeatedly, until there was little more than an assortment of oozing gashes, connected into a mangled puzzle of enzymes and viscera. A white t-shirt, smudged with sand, waded in the gory mess.

{VOID}

*KIRITSIS imagines what the collective death rattle of an untold number of sexually maimed children's souls would sound like, their lifeless eyes stitched shut, the inside lids fitted with acid dripping TV Screens that forever beam the grotesque grinning visage of a contemptuous giant rat straight into their smudged skulls, where the picture springs to flesh and blood and runs its filed talons in the creases of their brains, sporadically jamming them into the pleasure zones, so they are taught that the skinless nightmare wracking their spirits is actually something life affirming, something uplifting, something they've been wrong for avoiding. The screaming molested are now reborn into an incurably infectious Pavlovian litter, who are now in complete and utter control of the uninitiated. Teeth grow over their lips, poisoned millipedes live in their cremation-salted scalps, ink-spitting octopuses replace their hands, and always spring loaded in their shadows is a 6-foot rat, its face frozen in bland deadlight.*

I stopped to watch a mongrel bitch crouch behind a twitchy mutilated old junkie degenerate, lifting a wiry arm and tapping the inside of the elbow to bring out the vein. it tapped until the vein was as raised beneath the skin as humanely possible.

Nature would not have known these colors had we not been introduced to one another. So many shades of red and yellow and brown and black and red/yellow/black/brown mixes that no other tones exist. Even the brown is little more that red at its most dull... its most rusty.

the mongrel bitch began to lift the arm closer to its blistered goat-cunt face, the same time moving its face closer to the arm, until they met halfway, and wrapped its skirt-stripped lips around the area like a lover. You couldn't tell but afterwards that it had bit down, catching the vein between its teeth.

That was during the day... when the sodium lanterns bask us in imitation daylight. The nights are black-death oppressive. The streetlights go on, cutting into the black with a sharp, smooth white. When you walk under them, you appear as if in a high-contrast B&W photo; the shades and shadows as deep a chiaroscuro as the air, and the rest of your flesh is as white as the light.

the mongrel bitch pulled its incest-cum matted head back, the vein coming with it like rope being pulled by machines from under inches of wet tar. The vein snapped, and it began to floss, threading the vein through the spaces between its canines.

our suburb has turned into a micro-metropolis, with city-heavy traffic, houses rebuilt to look like compact apartment complexes, and even the most trivial places of business redesigned into towering infrastructures that seem to split the clouds until they are little more than an orbiting vapor, halos slipping down from heaven, sheathing over the concrete like condoms, leaving a thin trace of a once rich billow, making the cities look like giant graveyards from the set of a B-Movie.

The sky has been almost completely hidden behind bridges that connect the buildings, making the town look bleached from darkness. There are no trees or bushes or gardens, just sidewalks, streets, and buildings. The remaining plant life has grown around the buildings, thin twigs and vines coming in and out of sporadic cracks in the cement. This gives the structures a feeling of organic/inorganic fusion, referencing the new cold war: between "life" and "living". Children are born insane skunk ape vermin, left to their own devices by their hypnagogic subhuman caregivers, becoming cackling monstrosities that come to own the nights, which are uncharacteristically black, with wounded shocks of phased-out white from the newly installed streetlights. When one enters their spotlights, much of them is still a deep shade of black, with buried little bits of whiteness bringing out their details, becoming living B&W photographs of themselves. Much of the skunk ape vermin have adapted to this environment, and thus they are nocturnal, with heightened vision/senses in the night, and caramelized oil skin that is almost translucent, giving them an amphibious appearance, like giant salamanders bursting from anal wombs.

A large faction of the skunk ape vermin have been cutting the heads off matches for the past few months, putting them into large mayonnaise jars. At one point, a gang of skunk ape vermin brake into a facility housing an experimental breed of insect cocoons. they place this cocoons inside the throats of their breeding rat hosts. the cocoons hatch, with hundreds of tiny meat-eating butterflies spilling from the slimed husks. When they reach the back of their hosts eyes, they begin to gnaw away, until the eyes are completely gone and they can fly out of the sockets. parochial scum all run out into the streets in fits of pain, vomiting as butterflies now numbering in the thousands flutter violently from the hollowed-out eye sockets. With the butterfly swarm infesting in the area, the entire town is now under quarantine until the situation is under control, forcing the residents inside their homes.

One morning people wake up to find the jars lining the streets, each one filled to the tippy top with match heads.. Since they know who put them their, they keep them there, for fear of reprisal from the braying skunk ape vermin. They stay up that night, wondering what the skunk ape vermin will do the following night. That night comes, and the skunk ape vermin return, each one standing behind a jar of match heads. They are holding lighters, naked and seemingly coated in a fine glisten. They spark the lighters at the same time, placing the flame just about the top of the packed jars. the jars go up in a seconds-length burst of thick flames, which catch the skunk ape vermin's rectal-flecked skin, which turn out to be coated in gasoline. All the skunk ape vermin are now on fire, running through the streets, lighting up the night with the natural light of fire. Some catch the butterflies, cooking them in their hands. Some of them throw themselves into businesses, setting them all ablaze. The residents all leave there homes before the skunk ape vermin can burn them in their wreckage of their living quarters, and see everyone and everything as bright as it has ever been. They all stand in wonder, even as the filthy bodies of skunk ape vermin burn  right to the maggot-breeding bones.

In the morning, much of the tall buildings had burned almost to a black cinder, and for the first time in many years, a white sun hits the town.

- from *CERULEAN SWAN* by SKA (Apocatheid Books)

trees blushing gradients of liver-spotted copper. spitty hiss underscores the nursing. knife just about the nipple where a baby continues to suckle the tit. holds breast, milk and blood gushing heavily over baby head. knife placed between lips. scraping teeth on blade. chokes as some blood and milk falls off knife and down throat. takes baby in both hands, hovering backside over bladed mock-phallus. vague shadow of a baby impaled, blade popping out of their nape. reaches for handle of knife being held in mouth. digs into corners of mouth before slicing. top of head falls to ground. pull out of baby. body propped up by knees. plant baby head first into open throat-top.

*There were two beetles in KIRITSIS' room. one with wings and one without. dull gold in color. the wingless one clipped to the bottom of the winged one and they flew around the room. when caught, they separated, rolling onto their backs to play dead. in the stairway, clutching an issue of REVULSIONARY VIDEO magazine. KIRITSIS feels a kick in the sternum. he fell straight to the floor, by-passing the stairs and landing on his back. KIRITSIS could almost sense the rows of his spine breaking and rearranging themselves into an arbitrary design. as he lay there, totally winded, LYVERNE, KIRITSIS's babysitter, walks down the steps slowly. she stands over him and crouches down. then she clutches the sides of KIRITSIS' head and begins bashing him into the concrete floor. Since the wind had been knocked out of him, KIRITSIS was unable to scream. at some point LYVERNE began looking at the back of KIRITSIS' head every time she brought it up, to inspect the blow-pattern as it formed on the back of his skull. The harder she bashed, the larger the pattern grew. the larger the pattern grew, the softer was the sound of KIRITSIS head being smashed into the cement. Before too long the blows sounded like grapes under feet. KIRITSIS' eyes and teeth were completely red, as if all the blood from the back of his head been pushed forward and was now ready to burst from ripe cheeks and lips.*

a tornado of bats on fire spiral around the newly minted comic book goddess. clad in form fitting wet looking leather, zippers sporadically placed over her legs, abdomen, and chest, shaped like the grins of

Cheshire cats. her long icy black hair blows in semi-thick coils, obscuring every feature on her face but those sinfully beautiful eyes... like smoking gun metal. the bats dissolve in mid-air. Their still-smoking skeletons fall apart before they hit the ground, like a rain of tiny black bones. Ash cascades around her. She shakes the hair and debris from her face, maneuvering her cigar-burn red lips into a casually defiant sneer. She closes her eyes, stretches out her arms, and summons a wind powerful enough to lift her beyond the worlds.

doomsday cuck. heartless chuds get raped in piss. receiving oral sex from the victim of a curbing. the positive and the negative are equal in their capacity for toxic naivete. wave pool of salival fizz bulges the door's crack in a snaking lurch. the third line is believed to be known as an inside out jelly doughnut.

exactly what does it take to be noticed?

acknowledged?

validated?

relieved of this leaden desperation that churns the foam between my atoms?

selectors and rejectors.

flakes and frauds.

constant emotional whiplash.

{VOID}

faculties shaded by an exponentially darkening panic.

fuck out my skeleton through a human-shaped crack in the wall.

saying the word "crime" puts a taste in my mouth that's comparable to flame-seared ground-chuck sluicing a carefully toasted artisanal roll.

thoughts tumbling out in a readymade manifesto.

every impulse to be open and honest about the struggles registers as a libidinal postmortem.

dismissed as an "incel".

nah fuck those dudes.

i know the faults are mine.

the fractures, too.

you know a bit about that i reckon.

probably worse.

much much worse.

over more.

much, much more.

flippant dismissals consistent to the point of ambient bleeds and whispered ether.

**{VOID}**

let's just stop bothering each other.

let's just stop bothering ourselves.

let's just stop.

now put your nostrils into that "byeeeeeeee"

*KIRITSIS had heard of this spot in Hawntag... where a plume of hexavalent chromium from Gauntlean Water Power had settled at some point in the late nineties. it was around that time that the atmosphere of the area had shifted into something more at peace with accommodating the malignant phantasms undergirding the costume veneer of warmth and stability... when it let in the thrashing quivers of cosmic monstrosities, sacrificing the future on altars carved with dollar-sign runes and mossed with the gore of their regrettable offspring.*

*KIRITSIS had come to the conclusion that this plume was in fact a port of entry and exit for the malicious vassals of prehistoric ugliness that were once only confined to the unceasing night terrors of the psychologically misaligned. he had no concrete proof of this... just like he had no demonstrable evidence that authorities were closing in on him... but regardless, he made the plunge...*

... the bandages wrapped tight around my face can't prevent the dampening of my head-flesh as i plunge into the plume; its crackling pus wave skinning the blue tint off my goggles. i begin to sink in the snot-clacking abscess paste, soon finding out that this is only the crust of the plume.

i feel myself being sucked through a drain, piercing airs ushering me through a tunnel whose surface has been pimpled with the excreta of exploded living things, slashing my field jacket to ribbons, chopping the ribbons into confetti, blowing the confetti into particles.

eventually i am spat out into a room with no floor or ceiling, its colors an ever-shifting strobe of clashing ultraviolet and neon. i am momentarily suspended in midair, scanning a honey-comb of caverns and drainage pipes... their mouths carrion black behind archways of stalactites, gleaming like the needle-thin fangs of mastodonic worms.

i catch myself in a reflective surface; my bootleg *MANHATCHET* t-shirt saturated into a crude oil, the rips in the knees of the grey slacks reaching to the back of my legs, becoming cut offs with a sharp jerk, boots and gloves still intact, disheveled bandages like flat papery dreadlocks, only held in place by the goggles and gummy strips of duct-tapes that form an X around the shape of my head.

i once again feel myself being sucked forward, this time toward the gullet of a cave, its archway lined with broken antlers. the cobalt entrance of the cave turns out to be a waxy membrane damning the flow of a vertical pool. the last of my clothes are ripped away in this viscous current of what i can only assume are premature egg hatchlings that have been pureed into a blasting slush of meat, eyes, and bone.

i'm surging toward a metal grate, its bars warped into shapes that approximate the letters S, V, and K. i break through the grate, smearing the marble floor of a drained koi pond with a stretch of blue ink. my momentum halts in the middle of the pond, portions of the marble still arsenic green from stubborn algae-l blooms and gummed pennies.

i'm in the nerve center of a mall that has been abandoned by all but the proprietors, storefront displays still maintained and curated. an "urban" clothing store named Azure Charm has different Syrin Veda K videos playing on rows of televisions. the Welos Movie Theater has a standee of a creepily grinning egg-shaped woman set up at the entrance, an tie-in piece for the animated film *Lia DeFesisc and Mr. Nogoz and the Time Lia DeFesisc couldn't find Mr. Nogoz and Lia DeFesisc had to go looking for Mr. Nogoz.* the New Arrivals shelf at Sorebed Books has public domain pulp novel publisher Blue Rodent's "Vice Treasury" edition of *The Gloom; Bondage Phantom* and the latest from S. Delancey Allprick's unending *Wrathguild Tomes* universe, this time focused on the Sub-Crosser antagonist from the fourth *Skarsgroth* novel. the Eek! Toys has a joint diorama celebrating the dual relaunch of the

*Homunculords* line (renamed *Jumbo Mutanigains*) and a proper *Roboviolet Kaiju-Man* series, with Roboviolet Kaiju-Man sparring with Skabaurus the Mutanigen. off to the left of that display are the rather cheap-but-still-nifty Savage Brutality Wrestling action figures, with the "deluxe edition" Franco Sect figure dominating the eye. Re-Collector Comics has a shelf devoted to Cool Ranch Comics' new *Living Grave* miniseries, complete with the original Golden Age series collected in one volume. from an unsupervised kiosk selling bootleg Blu-Rays i catch a crude approximation of Sadisvalik, the villain from Deep Web Macumba's *Blue Gloom* series, apparently collected here in a single volume set... the case almost as thick as a book in the *Wrathguild Tomes* series.

on the floor above me, blocking the entrance of a Rases department store, there is a large head. its stare is that of an anonymous mask found in the crowd of a high society fuck ritual, lip-slit bolted shut with strips of chromium metal that form the shape of an X over the mouth, cheekbones streaked with candle wax tears that scar the imagination with an image of a wet melting face being pressed into the under grooves of a bleached pavement slab that had been molded into the countenance of a sneeringly blank mannequin.

on the marble floor of the drained koi pond there was something peeking from beneath a large layer of algae. i brushed the mold away with my foot, not at all concerned for the bacterial minutiae most likely teeming on its surface, and found an emblem that i had seen before; swords arranged into a grey star or rose with a dripping blue rodent skull in its center, its eyes gridded like those of a housefly, long crowded teeth curving and crossing over each other.

i looked back up and the giant face was now millimeters from my own, covered in glowing, bubbling runes that looked the letters S, V, and K merging into a single shape. its eyeholes erupted in geysers of greyscale mucus, flooding the consumerist ossuary unti....

*KIRITSIS awoke inside of an old car that had been parked in front of the Star Rose Mall, an endless 1990s hip-hop playlist on the car stereo. the House of Pain track "Legend" is queued up when he jostled awake by a knock on the window. KIRITSIS vibrates his head and pears up from the back of a station wagon. he's greeted by a pair of mustachioed detectives. they say their names are Norglam and Opastop.*

*KIRITSIS recognizes those names, and indeed their faces, from his grade school period in Hawntag. Orenthal Norglam and Neil Opastop; voted most likely to be the catalyst for the debilitating insecurities of a potential mass shooter. KIRITSIS recalls being at the receiving end of their reigns of terror up until about seventh or eighth grade, when he himself began growing into his future serial killer look.*

*one time, during their junior year, KIRITSIS snuck out from the Fracture Compound and infiltrated one of the clumsy orgies of the more "well-to-do" members of the student body politic. Norglam and Opastop were soused on foam from a dropped keg, thoughtless and loud to the point of violence, offering unprovoked, generalized but harsh criticisms of their classmates' looks and tastes, quizzing each other on what celebrities they would fuck (a sheepish young man blurted out "Lil' Kim" and was referred to by the epithet "nigger lover" by a perma-chuckling Opastop for the remainder of the night).*

*the duo were so self-enamored with their freshman boozer shenanigans that they didn't even notice their slightly above average girlfriends, who had once concussed phase one of KIRITSIS' emerging sexual identity with their "ironic" cat calling and full-volume laughter when speculation on his level of physical attractiveness would arise, had since reconsidered his appeal, and were now seemingly intrigued, if not torrid, when in his presence, which through years of group insult and social isolation had been pressurized into a hardened focus on the crust bejeweled amniotic fizz tethering those forces around him to the floating stain of unpolished loathsomeness that will always be our endgame.*

*"car is listed as belonging to a Shoshana Kiritsis. that*

*you?"*

*"my mother. i guess she lent it to me?"*

*"what for?"*

*"to go to the mall."*

*"for what?"*

*"probably the bookshop."*

*"'probably'?"*

*""'probably"""*

*Norglam and Opastop return their badges to their pockets, asking KIRITSIS to step out of the car. they don't seem to recognize him. they look tired; eyes puffy, mustaches crooked and bushy from lack of proper maintenance, suits that look slept in. KIRITSIS himself isn't much better for wear; a tropical shirt colored varying shades of blue worn over an egg white t-shirt with the phrase "THAT'S NOT GOOD I'M NOT HAPPY" written in midnight blue, grey work pants stiffened from absorbing a month's worth of secretions, and scratchy black wool socks. a pair of black Vans are shoved in the corner.*

*but its none of those things that have stirred the inquisition of central casting crime busters; it's the crumbled up body stocking and the tape-mouthed mask with runes cut into it, draped across the* passenger seat like the voided shedding of a bipedal lizard mime. the detectives' suspicions were further validated by the rune appearing to have been drawn across the forehead of KIRITSIS.

during this routine boost of mandatory quota, the meat-faced gumshoes had inadvertently stumbled upon "SHY GUY aka THE SURREAL KILLER" himself.

"Legend" goes into "Shook Ones Part 2" by Mobb Deep when the detectives snarling-ly demand KIRITSIS take them to "isolated dumping grounds". KIRITSIS, still fogged in a state of lingering deep sleep, is unsure of what they mean. they reach for KIRITSIS murder-skin and stick it in his face, volleying stock phrases from any number of Poliziotteschi films (Syndicate Vice Killers, Vincenzo Scapelli's sole foray into the genre, is a personal favorite of KIRITSIS'.).

KIRITSIS makes sure there is enough phlegm in his voice to marinate his cadence in the grit required to mock their gravely inflictions of speech, and tells them tells the detectives they'll need a boat. then he gives the relevant information.

the detectives cuff KIRITSIS and place him in their car. the direction they're headed in and the brievety of their drive suggests that aquatic transport has been arranged at a nearby bay.

{VOID}

*when they get on the boat, the ride is much longer. Norglam drives, while Opastop attempts to get KIRITSIS to open up about his motives, his pathos... more tired motions purloined from post-*Silence of the Lambs *Hollywood police procedurals. KIRITSIS quiet-talks a sardonic "let's not do that", to which Opastop replies with the sort of feigned incredulity left over from his beta-jock school days of sarcastic interrogation of his more unusual classmates.*

*"alright alright.. but what's with the outfit though?"*

"Sucker's Society."

*"huh?"*

"Sucker's Society *was a public access show that was on when we were kids. a variety show, with skits, cartoons, puppets etc. the host was "Sucker'; a clown made out of candy. well on some episodes, "Sucker" would be joined by "Choker"; his gloomy, unexitable twin sister. Sucker's color scheme was red and white like ribboned candy... get it?, Choker's was blue and grey. Choker's face was painted light blue, like that of a choking victim... get it? she also had big grey Xs painted over her mouth and eyes."*

*"pretty trippy."*

*"my mother played Choker for a few episodes."*

*"for real?"*

**{VOID}**

*"that's what she told me. before she introduced the show to me, she said she was the first actress to play Choker. this would've been when i was a baby."*

*"dad around?"*

*"never met him. i'm told he pops up from time to time."*

*"he got a name?"*

*"i remember hearing a 'C.R. Leon' being mentioned. never found any records or evidence of such a person existing."*

*"what's mom up to now?"*

*"not much. i don't see her often. she gets up and goes a lot. she had me when she was sixteen, y'know? always came back with comics and toys, though. she left me with some of her friends at the commune."*

*"she was in a cult?"*

*"something like that, yeah."*

*"i guess that explains the coded letters and knife attacks?"*

*"i told you... we're not doing that."*

*as Opastop resumes his "ain't this guy crazy" bad cop posturing, KIRITSIS leads the detectives under the Altomare bridge, grazing his fingers against the paint-chip spearheads of its rusted arch, to that floating stain on the ocean; the gated needle barge of Gromorrah. its shores are clustered with occupied body bags, the laconic grazing of the pulping skeletal faces blocked by cellophane muzzles.*

*the throats of the detectives resume their hemorrhaging glossolalia of cascading expletives, increasing both their blistering volume and intent-ful aggression. when they get close enough to the shore, detectives Norglam and Opastop jump into the dirty water, anxious to inspect the isolated dumping ground.*

*in their cop show haste, the detectives failed to detect that the water surrounding the island of Gromorrah is over-laced with a smorgasbord of chemicals. oils from the waste dissolve the cotton of their pant legs, lapping the flesh and muscle off their overworked shanks, singing the hair off the pasty staffs stressed with varicose from too much time spent on their feet.*

*the detectives make a beeline for the land, trying to dry off their legs in what they think is just another beachhead, but is in fact littered with dust mites, plastic shavings, and skin flakes.*

*KIRITSIS stays on the boat, running through probable insults he could sneer at his would be captors. when he can't settle on a kill shot more devastating than "i fucked your girlfriends", he forgo that portion of the formulaic ritual and went straight to the recitation a very specific Johnny Cash lyric, rendered in his best Tiny Tim falsetto;*

*"jailer, oh jailer / jailer, i can't sleep / cause all around the bedside / i hear the patter of Delia's feet"*

*roughly thirteen feet away from the detectives, a scab-scalped meat sack bubbles up from a steaming lagoon, its surface skinned with a soupy industrial grade vegetation. on her razored left cheek a cluster of benign cancers hang like frozen grapes consumed on the vine by noble rot. her figure is compact; stocky and wide, flesh sporadically raised with tea-stained gooseflesh. her breasts are tipped with segmented nipples, pointed into conical blades. her arms are black with hairs from her wrists to her elbows, a genetic motif that reprises down her lower extremities, giving the impression of wearing pants that have been tailored out of the chest of a dead horse.*

*MAITRESSE DELIA acknowledges KIRITSIS, offering a vague hint of forcibly polite recollection from his time spent at her Fracture Compound. not her most prized pupil, not one she is proud of, not even one she particularly likes, but one who's devotion to her is total, who will always breath her in until his lungs erode without end. the one who arguably best inhabits the cryptic ethos of SCAVILKADVRIS ; the endlessly perspiring voyeur entity that bore witness to the deicides whose blood and viscera served as a lubricant for the inaugural coupling of LYCANIVVE and JANRUMACH... the reclusive world builder whose own validating liquified outbursts remain forever braided in the fizzing trim of the viscous contents envenoming the DNA of the GOREGAZE.*

*MAITRESSE DELIA accepts the meager offering of these two warmed-over pulp novel tropes, dragging them by their brackish battered legs to be drowned and dissolved in the moat of stomach acid circling the Fracture Compound, where they thrashed and howled and convulsed as if being showered in boiling soup. after tumbling in the churn beneath the butane rainbow surface of the gastric vortex, one of the officers managed to remerge; the clothes and flesh melted into one vomit-swatch of pig roast headcheese, its hissing drip corroding holes in the bones of a skeleton the organ spring has softened to a lactic chaw.*

*there's a light pressure on KIRITSIS' shoulder.*

*"psstheyguesswhat?"*

*the dead world ASMR tone of RATLEY FUCHES has coiled into the ear drums of KIRTISIS like a cartwheeling potato bug.*

*"what is it, Ratley?"*

*"itiswhat."*

*RATELY FUCHES' bears his teeth, which are growing like weeds into blackish purple antlers that form the letters S, V, and K. his beady eyes rapidly clone themselves until the sockets appear occupied with the bulbing ocular grid of an enlarged jungle insect. the whole of his flesh peels backwards, forming a rose of grey swords that arrange themselves like sun rays around the back of his meat-faced countenance, which begins perspiring a fetal-clumpy azure mucus. the saturated vermin blossom spirals into the air, growing exponentially, until SCAVILKADVRIS can be brand its scarab on the egg-white film that jerks the curtain of the climatic limbo at the end of the multiverse.*

exploded pulp reconfigures into the shape of a woman, the skin toned like deep bruises covered in layers of bronzer in a fruitless attempt to mask their greening purple. the face is wet looking mound of clay. the eyes and mouth are shallow indentations... hastily scooped in by hand. the crooked vertical mouth is filled with teeth that resemble honey mustard pretzel pieces.... the eyes merely drawn onto the walls of the uneven sockets, creating the appearance of them being sucked by their gore to the back of the skull. a dollop of gelatinous mung has been spun across the scalp, sculpted into a swirling wave that parts just above where a left ear would be. in place of an ear, there is a cauterized branding wound... a now familiar crest reiterated by the healing process into a bubbled cables tangled into a gearwork of coiled-up potato bugs.

the halves of a vertically split baby head are like crescent phantom masks on the tits, the corners of exposed gums blending into the scar tissue seams at the edges of the areolas. her broiled legs are bound together, movements alternating between squirm and sway, a paraffin of toenails occasionally fanning the live nightcrawlers that have taken residence in the ash-powdered hollows left unoccupied when the labia was peeled.

the charbroiled prawn-nymph raises her arms, which look to be fashioned from extraneous thigh bones with thick balls of electrical tape acting as shoulders and joints, an opera glove of jaundiced wax stretched from the tip of the misplaced fingers to the bleeding root of the carotids, where they are laced into the neck with reams of garotte wire. grafted on each of the thumb spots are baby arms.. their skin caked with a gritty scum that occurs when dust particles collide with a tricky varnish... which thrash and claw seemingly independent of the rest of the body, like a pair of blown up carnivorous worms bursting from a sand dune that two decades of endless warheads have partially rendered a mirrored lake of glass.

lace remains simmer to phosphorus in a puritan voidscape. it can only be seen from the trichloroethylene-soiled rag pits at the chalked heart of Gromorrah: dead girls wrapped in plastic and thrown off a bridge float out to the middle of the ocean, where they clump into a garbage island.

they are the blue yolk of a long egg.

-------------------------------------------------

*One must still have chaos in oneself to be able to give birth to a dancing star.*

- Friedrich Nietzsche

*when the ritual, whatever form it takes, has been completed, then the killer often sinks into a kind of brief contentment during which his recent crime will be relived as fantasy until it no longer provides the stimulus the killer seeks. At this point, the hallucinations start again and we are back at the beginning, in the aura phase.*

From: *From Hell: Master Edition* by Alan Moore (pg. 32 of Appendix 1, Top Shelf Publications, 1996, 2020)

---

**AUBREY AURILEAN and SHOSHANA KIRITSIS will return in *GANGERS*.**

**For more about PIXY DEVILLE, please read *JeRk CuRtAiN* in *DARLING DELINQUENTS: AN ANTHOLOGY* from Sweat Drenched Press.**

-------------------------------------------

# SHY GUY TALES

## 1.

## GHOST APPLE

alright, hi. my name is Leanne Ronalds. this is the thirteenth meeting i've attended, but my first time speaking up.

listening to all of your truths has really helped in the processing of my ordeal, and i'm appreciative of your patience and understanding with respects to my initial hesitations to let you all in. you possess courage, wisdom, and resilience that i'm still not sure i have in me anymore... if it was ever there to begin with. but let's not get lost in the brush here, eh?

{VOID}

if we're going to start from the beginning, i guess we can trace this back to my cousin. we were real close growing up... like siblings and all that... playing *Asylum Thrashers* at the arcade, drawing cartoons, pretending we were a band in front of my uncle's camcorder, using kitchenware as makeshift instruments. things shifted when my uncle noticed some of his *Blue Rose Comics* were um.. "out of sorts" i guess we'll say... and we ended up not seeing as much of each other, due to my parents' concerns about my cousin and i looking over inappropriate material. nothing happened, but there was a brewing paranoia in the area at that time with regards to hardcore nudity or graphic violence cascading before the still shrink-wrapped peepers of "the children"... who grown-ups always seemed to talk about as an amorphous hive who responds to certain stimuli in the exact same way, but i digress.

my cousin and I drifted apart as teenagers do, but he kept plowing forward with his creativity. he did well enough for himself, but we could tell that he was perhaps spreading himself a bit too thin. he returned home for a visit... not sure if we were on the itinerary, but whatever... and he disappeared for a few days. he was found just a few minutes away from where we are now, totally fucking mutilated. they were only able to identify him by his tattoos.

when the media took hold of the story, they try to flush us out with money and air time. my parents and uncle barely waited for my cousin's formaldehyde treatments before taking the talk shows and magazines up on their offer, but i was a bit more selective in that field. of all the groups that did reach out to me, only one really piqued my curiosity enough to warrant a follow-through.

the gentleman said he and five others had formed an "elevated support group". they too had lost friends and loved ones in savage, brutal fashion, and they got two or three times a week to hang out, listen, and talk about whatever. i was assured that it wasn't a group... well, like *this* one, frankly... where we had to endlessly revisit and/or deconstruct our trauma, a practice which they believed only served in deepening stagnation.

the group started out well enough, but the shift happened so gradually none of us really noticed. one night we all just started rambling about our childhood obsessions; toys, games, movies, books, etc., which at some point morphed into the revelation that we had all at some point as kids created our own cartoon or comic book characters. we thought it might be fun to try and draw them from memory. subsequent meetings would evolve into us dressing as those characters. that escalated into us making a short film to be aired on late night cable access and the internet, which was designed to look like an infomercial for an MMA dojo, only we would be teaching kids how to be superheroes.

{VOID}

my character didn't really fit in with that milieu; a sentient marionette in Victorian Gothic garb who played the drums. when i first started drawing her as a kid, she didn't have a name, so for the benefit of the group i just called her "Doll Drums". i also added some cumbersome cyborg attachments to make her fit in with the others, who's characters and designs were more situated within the traditions of the superhero milieu.

we started a joke, but the two who founded the group told us that there was some genuine interest in making this "school of extreme altruism" a reality. i should let you know that no one else in the group ever received such inquiries, and when we asked the founders to elaborate they became cagey and evasive, so they were more than likely exaggerating or lying outright. they ended up buying some office space in a strip mall, and we started having our meetings there, always in full costume.

we lost the plot at a pretty rapid pace from then on out. the "school" amounted to little more than a den, where we played video games, smoked weed, or aimlessly talked shit about everyone and everything. if we got toasted enough, we might engage in some light BDSM activity... i guess if i'm being honest, that what this was for me; a kink. a chance to be weird and look hot and forget myself for a minute. i mean... "real life super heroes"? what part of fighting crime would ever find dressing up like half-destroyed ventriloquist dummy crucial to its effectiveness?

you know something... and this probably should fuck me up more than it does... i'm really not that broken up about what happened to them. i would've preferred not having to see what happened to them in real time, but now that i've had some distance to think on it, these people weren't really anything to me. whenever i would finally work up the nerve to be open and honest about my struggles, i was met with the sort of terse aloofness that quietly rude late-term adolescents show to lonely elders who attempt harmless small talk. slowly the understanding creeped up on me; these people haven't actually lost anyone or anything... or if they did, they didn't care beyond using it as excuse to be reckless, cynical, and awful to themselves, each other, and those who occupy their immediate orbit, softening the blow by draping their egocentrism in a half-ass indulge-ment of misguided nostalgia. i mean... one of these maggot-dicked fuckmouths turned out to be a member of a white power terrorist cel, y'know?

i mean.. i fucking lived, right? they don't have to bear the dampening weight of this onset putrescence any longer. i watched it. all of it. i followed his rules. "look forward", "try nothing", "first one to break gets broken"... i might be experiencing a bit of the old Mandela Effect with that last line... like how i can't remember if his head was wrapped in bandages... if the emblem he had written on his coat reprised in a cypher across those bandages... or if he was wearing the kind of temperature-control mask that marines wear in climates of extreme cold, only dipped in white varnish.

the PTSD has a way of editing it all down a smash-cut jumble of rope-snapping, quizzical head-tilts, coarse gargling, and hacking motions. memories settle to humming quietude after he finishes. i was tied up, laying on my belly... the ropes weren't too tight, as he had us do the tying, which none of us were very good at, but nevertheless i let him think me bound. he suddenly got bashful; playing with his face, directing head motions towards his shoulder, swatting at it as if it were being nudged without consent by an invisible hand. the last thing he said to me was a struggle to decipher, as he spoke in an unbroken mumble, but it sounded like "alright do what you want".

i'm a lot like i've been since it all happened. locked up in storage. roiling internally at a frustrating loss to articulate the visions without its expression coming forward as more than a ballistic warble of labyrinthian resentment. surface molecules frozen in place. meat and bone coordinating their rot, becoming a marbled olive liquid that slips through a crack at the feet, leaving a diamond husk in my public shape... a haunted doll carved from an ice-shell, twirling in the air as if attached to a mobile of hanging victims.

{VOID}

thanks again.

----------------------------------------------

# SHY GUY TALES

## 2.

## SPRINGTIME INSECT

**HE LOOKS** exactly the way i thought he'd look. gaunt and sunlight-averse, eyelids puffing into a purplish amphibian neck sack-bloat, a ring of grime-slicked hair falling like damp moth eaten curtains from beneath the cobweb brim of a dissolving fedora, leaving grey stains on the shoulders of his oversized half-buttoned dress shirt. there is a theatrically laconic cadence sluicing his words with practiced apathetic dread, as if left weary by the restless Armageddon perpetually bursting within his caustic imagination.

{VOID}

"okay, so... here's the skinny handsome. the message boards on my page here? they keep going on about these 'Shy Guy' attacks. have you heard?"

"yeah... at that law office, right?"

"very good then. yeah right so this cat burst into a office and cut up some old bitches with a machete, wearing an outfit that my users say resembles a character from some video game named... wait for it... 'Shy Guy'."

"yeah it's from *Super Mario Brot...*"

"*Super Mario Brothers TWO*! yeah that's the ticket. anywhooo... the commentary has been gnawing at me for a minute here. see... i've hit a bit of a wall creatively... the new material for the site just hasn't been up to snuff... hehehehe oh shit get it... 'snuff'? didn't mean to do that swearsies. so after pouring over the theories and stories and essays and think pieces about this 'Shy Guy', i finally stumbled upon an idea that's been gesticulating in my mind since i was a kid. y'know those old film serials?"

"you mean like *Flash Gordon* or *Fear Woman?*"

"you're on the trolley... um.... i'm sorry how to i say your name again?"

"Thigh-la-sin"

"Thylacine! cool. hi i'm Daxis."

**{VOID}**

"so what about those old film serials then?"

"right. so yeah, what if we did some kind of chapter play, only instead of revolving around a superhero or a secret agent, it revolved around the exploits of a 'Machine Man' type."

"'Machine Man'?"

"oh whoops, you know how in a lot of faux snuff films, the acts are usually carried out by some masked and/or hooded beefcake? well that archetype is often referred to as a Machine Man. usually they look pretty interchangeable, like an executioner or a leather daddy, wearing black, etc. well what if we fused that type with the more defined aesthetic of a super-villain. see i was thinking a blue latex body suit... with a sleeve where the cock could go... and a white mask with a zipper-mouth in the shape of an X... cause this 'Shy Guy' killer had tape Xing out the mouth of his mask, ya dig?"

Daxis keeps talking through me, as if he's aiming for his words to peel the paint off the walls of his office, located somewhere adjacent to the bowels of this building. to myself i'm thinking alright... this is different, but i'm feeling it a bit. i used to run around with a lot of 'Real Life Superhero' types, which was really just a variation on the costume fetish community i've been heavily involved with since my late teens. i liked playing the villain... especially when my "arch-enemy" was a mouthwatering ball of muscle named "Rawdog". wonder what happened to that guy.

"alright, so here's the general outline; you'll be playing 'SadisValiK', our main character, who breaks into the home of our nameless victim, played by Mona Grub. you're into girls, right? i know you mostly work in the gay market, so i need to know right now if you'll be able to maintain an erection with a girl."

"yeah i can fuck with girls just fine, Mr. Daxis."

"i had a feeling, just had to be sure. i'll leave the details of the aktions up to you too, but she's more than likely game for whatever you want. choking, hanging, throwing against a wall, slamming through a floor, getting whipped bloody, pumping her holes with tricky substances, punching... oh man, she's really into the punching... especially on a full stomach. she either feels nothing or is really top flight at compartmentalizing her pain... either way, ever since the *Springtime Insect* vignette, she's been a real favorite among the users. and don't tell her i said this... but she picked you out of line up, which means that you and her can *really* can go to those dark places. i'm serious, Thylacine... *BLUE GLOOM* could be Deep Web Macumba's masterpiece."

i've seen the *Springtime Insect* scene with Mona Grub. as i can remember it goes like this; Mona drizzles a sponge of honeycomb across her tongue, tits, ass, and cunt. she is then approached by two large women, one wearing a mosquito mask and the other wearing a mantis mask. the bug-headed dykes proceed to spit-roast Mona with hollow glass strap-ons that have been filled with live bees, turning the dildos into no-batteries-required vibrators. after this section cycles through some multiple orgasms, there is a smash cut to Mona on her back, with her asshole in the air. the bug-headed dykes gape Mona's asshole with large forceps. hold it open with spider-shaped speculums, and dump a cracker box full of cicada shells into the dilated rectal cavity. the camera lingers for what feels like thirteen minutes on the cicada shells, its lens being drawn deep into a mass grave meat tunnel.

pretty intense stuff, but i think we can outdo it. physically she's quite the anomaly with regards to this genre of violet pornography... foxy and radiant, with none of the washed out, numb-around-the-heart aloofness that accompanies many of the actresses in this corner of the medium, who always appear to be under a black spell of shotgun duress. something about Daxis tells me his libidinal preferences lie within the hostage aesthetics of squeezing victimization (and if i'm being candid, mine do as well) , but in order to expand his base of operations, he is acquiescing to the conventional demands of the wider pornography market, while still hoping to maintain the bleeding edge of depravity that extended his invitation to this brutal dance of escalating extremes.

"but no pressure, right?"

"heh... you're the boss, applesauce."

**I'M FITTED** for the "SadisValiK Skin", as Daxis calls it. it's a vascular latex body suit, colored a midnight blue, with some talons fashioned from some kind of lightweight metal sewn between the layers of the fingers.

the hood droops from the throat like skull-voided flesh, egg white leather, mesh orbs bubbling from the eye sockets, resembling the peepers of a predatory bug. the mouth is a pair of zippers overlaid to form an X, with one zipper opening the leather layer of the head and the other zipper opening the wire mesh undergirding of the mask.

there is a long cobalt sock below the navel of the suit, its length a rather generous assumption of my length and girth, with a maneuvering of the slack the material ends up offering snug accommodations for my steadily ramping engorgement.

after i'm adjusted, i signal for Daxis to enter the modest dressing room.

"kid... you look fucking fa-boo."

not exactly the term i was expecting, being that when i look in the mirror all i see is some kind of wrongheaded gene-splicing between a sleep paralysis hallucination and a vigilante rapist from a Japanese porn comic... but i guess considering who i'm working with here, i suppose it should be expected.

"alright, well here's the set-up, chief. our girl Mona is going to be laying on the couch in front of this open window, thumbing through some French literature, ya dig? well i figured she can maybe jerk herself off for a bit... i know i know... basic shit, right? anyway, you'll be creeping in front of the window, staring holes into the room. then you'll reach through the window and drop those clawed mitts where her shoulders end and her neck begins. then you just fucking ragdoll this nasty cunt, right? i mean like, clip her head on the ceiling fan, right?"

"maybe if she wears her hair up in a pony tail, i can knot it around one of the blades of the ceiling fan? have her spin around, maybe it'll even dislodge from the fixture and rip a hole in the ceiling, and i can thrust her up into the hole?"

"not bad. if i could figure out of way for her to be stuck in the ceiling hole, then you could treat her like a heavy bag."

it's more than likely that none of this will work even a little, but it's good to get all the wild shit out of you, as long as you retain the knowledge that it will probably be compromised as its dragged before the gaze of the lens.

**SHE DIDN'T** want to meet me before i slipped into the skin. i wonder if this was her request or at the insistence of Daxis, as he made it clear that he wanted an accurate terror reaction on the part of Mona.

"look dude, Mona picked you out of a line-up like i said, right? but the thing is i never really told her exactly who would be wearing the SadisValiK skin. i like her not knowing... and deep down, i think she does, too. i know she looks all warm and bubbly, but i have never worked with someone this hardcore in all my years on the scene. i'm not pulling pud here, 'malright? the girl can be ruthless. and who's the boss?"

"applesauce?"

"you got it. now let's remind that fucking pig of bottomless thirst who runs this shit."

i can no longer tell where theatrical motivation ends and spiteful malice begins, but i can't help but feel ready to physically scarify, emotionally lacerate, and intellectually annihilate a beautiful stranger who wanted to get paid to have me fuck them, and in the process skull-rape cavernous fissures into the eyeholes of the morose onlookers whose deepening prurience has led them to this caustic netherworld of fleeting power and debilitating humiliation.

"you're the boss, applesauce."

------------------------------------------------------

## NO GAME, NO SHAME.

## - N.

*come find me:*

http://masochistian.blogspot.com/

http://scumgristle.tumblr.com/

http://fetalgoathusk.blogspot.com/

soundtrack available here: http://fetalgoathusk.blogspot.com/2021/01/soundtrack -for-ancient-ones-shy-guy.html

# Author's Bio:

N. Casio Poe lives and operates out of Long Island, New York.

From 2004 – 2008 he was the vocalist/lyricist for the grindcore band THE COMMUNION.

His previous works include PIECEMEAL, TERSE (Sweat Drenched Press) and the short stories LYCANTHROPY WIFE, JERK CURTAIN, and THE FLOATING STAIN have appeared in USERLANDS (Little House on the Bowery), DARLING DELINQUENTS (Sweat Drenched Press) and THE AGON JOURNAL (respectively).

He continues to write.

Head over to:

https://sweatdrenchedpress.webador.co.uk/order-1

and order directly via the Press to ensure better royalties and the continuation of our innovative Press.

Also, please don't forget to leave a review on Goodreads, Amazon & wherever you leave reviews.

**{VOID}**

Printed in Great Britain
by Amazon